'You reach

Lisa bit her lip,
Her temper had
liable to run awa__   __t was more
than time she lea____ __o control.

'I apologise,' she said.

'Lip-service.' Brett was giving no quarter. 'But we'll let it pass—this time.' He watched her face, accurately judging the struggle going on inside her. 'Is it just me who rubs you up the wrong way, or are you always this prickly?'

Dear Reader

It's the time of year when nights are long and cold, and there's nothing better than relaxing with a Mills & Boon story! To help you banish those winter blues, we've got some real treats in store for you this month. Enjoy the first book in our exciting new LOVE LETTERS series, or forget the weather outside and lose yourself in one of our exotic locations. It's almost as good as a real winter holiday!

The Editor

Kay Thorpe was born in Sheffield in 1935. She tried out a variety of jobs after leaving school. Writing began as a hobby, becoming a way of life only after having her first completed novel accepted for publication in 1968. Since then, she's written over fifty and lives now with her husband, son, German shepherd dog and lucky black cat on the outskirts of Chesterfield in Derbyshire. Her interests include reading, hiking, and travel.

Recent titles by the same author:

A RECKLESS ATTRACTION
WORLDS APART

TRIAL IN THE SUN

BY
KAY THORPE

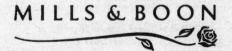

MILLS & BOON

MILLS & BOON LIMITED
ETON HOUSE, 18-24 PARADISE ROAD
RICHMOND, SURREY TW9 1SR

First published in Great Britain 1994 by Mills & Boon Limited

© Kay Thorpe 1994

Australian copyright 1994   Philippine copyright 1995 This edition 1995

ISBN 0 263 78819 9

Set in Times Roman 10 on 12 pt. 01-9501-52811 C

Made and printed in Great Britain

CHAPTER ONE

'CASH!' demanded the swarthy Puerto Rican. 'You give cash!'

Trying to look and sound calm and confident, Lisa shook her head. 'I don't have any on me.'

It had been a bad idea coming out on her own at this hour of the evening; she knew that now. Main thoroughfare or not, there were few other people on foot, and no one else at all in the immediate vicinity.

'You give cash,' repeated the man threateningly. 'Or I take!'

She was telling the truth, but he obviously didn't believe her. Heart thudding sickeningly against her ribcage in recognition of her danger, Lisa attempted to break to the side in an effort to slip past him and make a run for it, but he forestalled her, seizing her roughly about the waist and clapping a sweaty hand over her mouth as he began pulling her towards a darkened alley a few feet away. If he once got her in there, anything could happen, she thought frantically, but her struggles made no impression.

It took the sudden screech of brakes at the kerbside to pull him up. Another male voice shouted something and next moment she was thrust aside, stumbling to her knees as her would-be captor disappeared into the alleyway.

Too shaken to move for a moment or two, Lisa was vaguely aware of approaching footsteps. She shrank involuntarily from the firmness of the hand that came under her elbow to draw her back to her feet.

'You're in no danger from me,' said her rescuer on a dry note. 'Are you hurt at all?'

'Not physically,' she acknowledged, making an attempt to regain some degree of dignity. 'Just a little unnerved.'

'Hardly surprising. You came within an ace of rape—or worse!'

'He was only after money,' she said, and saw the well-defined mouth take on a slant.

'Of course. Blue-eyed blondes are in such ready supply here.' He gave her no time to reply—if there was a reply to be made. 'Where are you staying?'

He was taking it for granted that she was a tourist, but then why wouldn't he? Lisa asked herself wryly. Who else but a tourist would be doing what she had been doing?

'The Ambassador Plaza,' she said.

Dark brows lifted. 'That's some distance away.'

'I came out for a walk,' she admitted, 'and got a bit lost.'

'A walk? In San Juan!' The sarcasm cut to the quick. 'Are you totally naïve, or just plain reckless?'

'Neither,' she returned with some acerbity of her own. 'I made a mistake, that's all.'

'One which might have cost you dearly.' He indicated the long low limousine waiting at the kerbside. 'I'll take you back to the hotel.'

There was a uniformed chauffeur in the driving seat, Lisa noted, which made the possibility of maybe jumping from the frying-pan into the fire unlikely. Refusal in the circumstances would be foolish. She wasn't even all that sure in which direction the hotel lay.

The man took her agreement for granted, urging her ahead of him into the rear of the car, then sliding in beside her. 'The Ambassador Plaza,' he instructed the driver.

Settling back into the soft leather, he turned an appraising gaze on Lisa, who was far from relaxed in the luxurious confines, taking in every detail of her finely boned oval face beneath the bell of corn-gold hair.

'How old are you?' he asked unexpectedly.

Lisa bridled a little at the presumptuous question, but couldn't find it in herself to tell him where to get off in the circumstances.

'Twenty-three, if it's of any importance,' she said shortly.

'Old enough to have acquired some common sense. I'd advise a little more application of it if you want to see twenty-four. Women can't afford to take chances even in England these days.'

Lisa cast a sideways glance as he turned his head to look out of the window. English born himself, she judged, although not recently domiciled there if the deep tan of the lean features, discernible even in street-lighting, was anything to go by. He would be in his mid-thirties, at a guess, with an air of command about him. There was a certain arrogance too in the way he had taken her to task. Grateful as she was for his help, his attitude rankled.

Damping down aggression, she took her cue from the white dinner-jacket he was wearing to murmur politely, 'I hope I'm not making you late for whatever it is you're on your way to.'

His shrug was brief. 'A few minutes perhaps. I take it you're travelling alone?'

'Yes,' she admitted, and then with a faint defiance, 'I like travelling alone. It means I can do what I want to do and see what I want to see in my own time.'

'You could do that still with compatible companionship. You're obviously unmarried, and two women travelling together are scarcely safer than one, but you must have men friends who'd be willing to accompany you.'

'None I'd want with me,' Lisa retorted crisply. 'Anyway, I shan't be taking any more risks from now on, so you don't need concern yourself.'

'There are better places to spend a holiday than Puerto Rico,' he commented, ignoring the last. 'You should try one of the smaller islands.'

That was exactly what she would be doing as from tomorrow, and not on holiday, but she saw no reason to tell him so. They were already drawing up in front of the brightly lit and blessedly recognisable frontage of the hotel where she was spending the night, much to her relief. The sooner she was out of this man's presence the better.

He got out of the car in order to let her out on to the pavement, topping her by half a foot at least when she straightened. His shoulders were broad beneath the superbly tailored dinner-jacket, tapering down to a narrow hipline, the whole impression one of leanly muscled fitness. Few women could fail to be aware of his masculine attraction, Lisa conceded, feeling the involuntary flutter in the pit of her stomach. Nor, she was sure, was he unaware of it himself.

'Thank you again,' she said on a slightly husky note. 'I'm...very grateful for your help.'

The dark head inclined, grey eyes revealing a hint of mockery. 'Glad to be of service. Take care.'

Lisa heard the car pull away as she went into the hotel, but she didn't look back. The lobby was well-populated with people both coming and going, many of them dressed for the sophisticated nightlife on offer in modern San Juan. There was music coming from the direction of the bar, and a glimpse through the open doors of a thronged clientele. Too many people and too much noise for her, Lisa thought, making her way to the lifts. With an eight o'clock flight, she would need to be at the airport by seven-thirty at the latest, so a reasonably early night seemed advisable anyway.

Closing the door of her spacious and luxuriously equipped room some moments later, she could still scarcely believe her continuing good luck. Held up for an hour in New York, and consequently arriving in San Juan to find her connection for St Thomas already flown, she had accepted the airline's offer of a hotel for the night with trepidation, more than half anticipating some flea-pit in the suburbs, certainly nothing like this.

Her eventual destination would be even better, of course. The Isle Royale hotel was reputed to be one of the finest in the Caribbean. Judging from the brochure she had seen, it certainly had to be one of the most expensive! There was no way she could ever afford to stay in a place like that, but working there would be almost as good.

Resident masseuse to a clientele accustomed to the very best in life would be no easy ride, for sure, although she had no doubts as to her ability to provide the kind of treatment that would be expected. Her training and subsequent salon experience had been top class too. Gary Conway had been impressed enough to offer her the job, which was a confidence booster in itself. A three-month trial period with the very real possibility of an extended contract at the end of it was surely worth going out on a limb for. The season down here was all year round, with sunshine most days. That one fact alone was a draw.

It was only after she was in bed, listening to the faint sound of music coming from the lower reaches, that her thoughts returned to the man who had rescued her. That he was one of the monied class was more than obvious. A gentleman in one sense, she supposed, yet with the kind of dominating manner that aroused every warring instinct in her. A man, she reckoned, who saw all women as empty-headed inferiors in need of protection from their own follies. True, her own behaviour tonight had done little to discredit that theory, but one learned from one's mistakes.

As there was little if any chance of her bumping into him again, it scarcely mattered what he thought of her, she told herself firmly at that point, dismissing the incident from mind. A good night's sleep was what she needed.

She was awake at six, and back at the airport before seven. Asked by the check-in clerk if she would like to take the earlier flight at seven-fifteen, she accepted with alacrity, and followed directions to the appropriate gate, where several other people were already waiting for the ticket steward to lead the way out to the small island plane.

Lisa tagged on behind a family party of four who appeared to be dressed for a day trip in shorts and T-shirts. Which was exactly right, she gathered from snatches of conversation overheard during the following few minutes.

Someone else came up at her back, and she half turned to direct a friendly glance, the smile freezing on her lips as she looked up into those grey eyes again. By daylight he seemed even taller, his shoulders broader than ever in the pale blue shirt open on the taut, sun-bronzed column of his neck. One eyebrow lifted quizzically as he viewed her.

'So you took my advice,' he said.

'Not really,' Lisa denied, recovering. 'I was heading for St Thomas in any case.'

'That wasn't the impression I had last night.'

Her shrug was deliberate. 'Then it was obviously the wrong one.'

'So it appears.' He sounded amused. 'Whatever, I approve.'

'I'm so glad.' Her own tone was honey-sweet. 'Are you just visiting the island yourself?'

He shook his head, the amusement in no way decreased. 'I live there. At least, part of the time I do. How long are you planning on staying?'

'Three months to start with.' Lisa registered the surprise in his eyes and judged its cause. In her cotton trousers and sleeveless top, she no doubt looked far from the class of tourist able to afford extended stays anywhere. An explanation trembled on her lips, but she bit it back. It was no one's business but her own.

With everyone travelling on the flight apparently now present, the steward opened the glass doors and beckoned them all through, taking tickets as they passed. Lisa moved smartly, but found herself unable to outpace the man following on. She kept her gaze fixed firmly to the front as he drew level.

'I gather it's your first trip to these parts?' he said conversationally. 'Few people stay more than a week or so on any one island. They all have their attractions.'

'It's surely a matter of choice,' Lisa answered. 'I like to concentrate on getting to know one place well rather than several fragmentarily. I'm sure I'll find plenty to occupy me on St Thomas. The sun is a bonus in itself, coming from an English November.'

'Foggy and damp.' His tone was reminiscent. 'I can't blame you for wanting to get away from it for a while.'

'How long is it since you were in England?' she asked curiously.

'Several years,' he acknowledged. 'And then only for a matter of days. I was thinking back to when I was a boy. My family moved out here when I was twelve.'

'To St Thomas?'

He shook his head. 'Tortola.'

That was one of the British Virgins, Lisa knew. She wondered if they were there still, but didn't feel inclined to ask any further questions.

The plane was a twin-engined propeller type which looked as if it had seen long service. Lisa reassured herself with the thought that it must make the forty-minute journey between the islands several times a day without mishap. She had a window seat, and was none too delighted to find her erstwhile companion taking the aisle seat next to her.

'Home in time for breakfast,' he said lightly. 'Are you renting, or staying in a hotel?'

'Hotel,' Lisa answered, then, anticipating the next question, 'The Isle Royale.'

'For three months?' This time his tone was verging on scepticism. 'I take it you do have a reservation?'

There was little point in hedging any further, Lisa concluded resignedly. He obviously knew as well as she did the unlikelihood of anyone short of a millionairess spending three months in a hotel of the Isle Royale's class.

'As a matter of fact, I'm not there as a guest,' she admitted. 'I'm on the staff.'

'Really?' The dark brows had drawn together. 'In what capacity?'

'Resident masseuse.'

The starting of the engines smothered his verbal response to that piece of information, but if his expression was anything to go by it hadn't been all that encouraging, though she failed to see why.

'The job was advertised in England?' he asked as the engine noise smoothed out a little.

'Well, no.' It was hardly his concern, but Lisa still felt under some obligation from last night. 'The hotel's general manager pulled a muscle jogging through St James's Park during a visit to London last month. I happened to be in the vicinity, and managed to ease it for him.'

'And he offered you a job on the spot?'

'Not right there and then. He came to the salon where I worked for further treatment.'

'Expensive sessions, no doubt?'

'No more than most.' Lisa was beginning to resent the tone of this conversation—if it could be called that.

They were gathering speed down the runway now. She put her head back against the rest, not really trusting the two propellers to provide enough power for lift-off. It was the first time she had flown in anything but jets.

However, take-off was smoother than anticipated. They lifted to what seemed like no more than a few hundred feet before flattening out over a sea of brilliant aquamarine shading to deepest blue where it ringed the scattered offshore islands. Lisa gazed fascinated at the spreading scene, relishing the sunshine, the vivid colours,

the whole idea of being here in the Caribbean at all—
light-years away from the world she had left behind.

The man at her side had fallen silent. When she did
finally steal a glance at him, he was looking straight
ahead, face expressionless. A strongly chiselled profile,
forehead high and intelligent beneath the crisply styled
dark hair, nose jutting straight as a die, lips firm and
well-shaped, jawline clean-cut. She wondered who and
what he was. So far, he knew more about her than she
about him.

Not that it really mattered when it came right down
to it. Whoever he was, they were hardly going to be
moving in the same circles.

He maintained the silence during the rest of the
journey. Coming in to land, Lisa was too taken up with
the scenery to worry about touch-down: rolling green
hills, strips of dazzling white sand beaches, pastel-
coloured buildings. She was going to love it here, she
knew. Who could fail to?

Her companion was first on his feet when the plane
came to a final standstill, reaching up into the overhead
locker to bring down her carry-on bag along with his
own folded garment carrier.

'Thanks,' she said, taking the bag from him.

His smile was perfunctory. Since discovering her true
status in life, his whole attitude had undergone a distinct
alteration, Lisa reflected. She wouldn't have had him
down as that type, but first impressions were often
wrong, as she had found to her cost in the past. People
were people in her estimation, no matter how much
money they happened to have. Those who considered
themselves a cut above the rest because of it weren't
worth a second thought anyway.

There was a short walk across the tarmac in a heat already building into the upper seventies, to a small but surprisingly modern terminal building. Having gone through Customs last night at San Juan, Lisa was able to go straight through to Baggage Reclaim along with those of the other passengers not merely here for the day. The man she had travelled with went off in the direction the rest were taking. No great loss, she told herself. Hopefully, that was the last she would see of him.

The baggage came through after what seemed an interminably long wait. 'Caribbean time,' explained the man she asked if it usually took this long. 'Everything moves at its own pace here. You either accept that, or blow a gasket trying to beat it.'

Lisa laughed. 'I think I can live with a slower pace. It will make a nice change.'

'Until you need something doing urgently,' came the somewhat wry response.

For herself she could think of nothing that might call for immediate action, though time, she supposed, would tell. For the present she resolved to adopt the same easy-going attitude to life.

Her two suitcases were heavy, and there appeared to be neither porters nor trolleys available. Head down as she trudged doggedly in the direction of the taxi signs, she failed to see the man approaching until he loomed right in front of her.

'I'll take those,' he said. 'I have transport waiting.'

'It's quite all right,' Lisa assured him, unable to keep the asperity from her voice. 'I can manage, thank you.'

'At the risk of having to treat your own strained muscles, I dare say you can,' he returned drily. 'Hardly

worth it for the sake of making a point, is it? I'm going
to the Royale myself.'

'I thought you said you lived here?' she queried.

'Only part-time. When I am here I live at the Royale.'

A regular guest. That perhaps explained his interest
in her appointment. Not that it excused the tone of his
questioning.

'I can take a taxi,' she said, reluctant to be under any
further obligation.

'Taxis don't come cheap here. Very little does.'

'I'm not exactly a pauper,' she flashed. 'I can afford
it.'

There was no element of apology in his regard. 'But
as we're going to the same place you don't need to.
Accept the offer with good grace.'

Other than to show herself in a very bad light by telling
him what he could do with his offer, there was little else
for it but to accept, Lisa acknowledged wryly as he took
the suitcases from her and turned back the way he had
come.

The transport proved to be a gleaming new Dodge
people-mover, its driver a young West Indian who greeted
the two of them with a wide smile and an air of easy
familiarity. It was only on seeing other, similar vehicles
dropping and picking up passengers further along that
she realised this was one of the general island taxis
anyway.

'Don't you have any other luggage?' she asked her
benefactor curiously as they drew away from the terminal, having noted the lack of suitcases other than her
own in the rear compartment.

'I travel light,' he said. 'The name's Sanderson, by
the way. Brett Sanderson.'

'Lisa Renshaw.' She made an effort to adopt an appropriate attitude. 'This is very kind of you, Mr Sanderson.'

There was irony in the inclination of the dark head. 'As I said, I was going your way. You'll see the Royale up above the town when we get round the hill. It's a couple of miles to the nearest beach, but the Charlotte Amalie harbour view is what most people come for. It's reputed to be one of the four finest in the world, especially at night.'

Having already seen pictures of it in the travel books she had perused with such interest during the past few weeks, Lisa could well believe it. Tonight she would be seeing that same view first hand, and on many more nights to come. She was going to make a success of this job, she vowed silently, no matter what!

An old-world town climbing from the shoreline into the surrounding emerald-green hills, Charlotte Amalie had all the Caribbean atmosphere she had missed in San Juan. She could name several landmarks from her studies, such as the pale green legislature building on the waterfront and the sturdy red bulk of Fort Christian which had once protected early colonists from foreign intruders. Beyond and above lay the red-roofed sprawl of Bluebeard's Castle hotel, built around an old stone tower supposedly home to the legendary pirate. Higher still, sparkling white against the green, the long, low curve of the Isle Royale hugged the hillside.

Turning off from the waterfront, they took a steep and narrow road which wound up through wooded slopes for several minutes, to pass finally through an imposing arched gateway into beautifully landscaped grounds. Two long, rodent-like brown animals foraging among the vividly flowered shrubbery lining the driveway paid little heed to the passing vehicle.

'Mongooses,' said Brett Sanderson as Lisa twisted in her seat to look back at the pair. 'You'll see plenty of those. Iguanas too, if you keep your eyes open, although the best place is around Limetree Beach further along the coast.'

The drive made a final turn and flattened out beneath impressive colonial portals. Alighting from the vehicle, Lisa drank in the superb view out over the whole harbour and outlying islands. There were three cruise liners tied up at the wharf way down on the left, while beyond spread a multitude of smaller craft at anchor across the blue-mirrored bowl. The distances were already misted in heat, the sky cloudless but for a mere puff or two of white way out over the sea. The light breeze carried the mingled scents of jasmine and hibiscus.

'It's even better in life than in print!' she exclaimed with genuine enthusiasm. 'I can hardly believe I'm really here!'

'It's no dream,' Brett Sanderson assured her. 'Although if you'd been here a few years ago when Hugo struck, you might have considered it a nightmare.'

Lisa turned back to look at the solid stone frontage of the hotel. 'I can't see any signs of hurricane damage.'

'The Royale was built the year after, but the island as a whole took a battering.'

The driver had taken her bags from the car and deposited them on the front step. Another young islander dressed smartly but comfortably in white trousers and yellow shirt came out from the hotel interior to pick up both suitcases, face creased in a welcoming smile.

'I'll take these right through to Reception, ma'am,' he said, and disappeared swiftly inside again before Lisa could protest.

Brett Sanderson turned from paying off the taxi driver, and indicated the open doors. 'Shall we go in?'

As staff, she would hardly be checking in at the main desk, Lisa thought, but she could only take her cue from him. No doubt he would point her in the right direction once they were indoors. She felt the brush of his bare forearm against hers as he moved at her side, and knew a sudden electric tingle under her skin. Simple chemistry, she told herself. Whatever else he might or might not be, he exuded masculinity from every pore.

The hotel lobby put that of the Ambassador Plaza in the shade. Marble-floored and superbly furnished, it had whirring fans set into the high ceiling and a preponderance of lush plant life. Straight out of a Somerset Maugham novel, reflected Lisa admiringly, eyes following the lovely sweep of a staircase.

She smiled in relief as she dropped her gaze again to see the familiar features of the man making his way towards them. At forty-two—or so he had told her—and retaining a full head of hair, Gary Conway was still a very attractive man. As general manager of a place like the Isle Royale, he had every reason to be proud.

'Hello!' she greeted him. 'I got here at last!'

'Good.' He both looked and sounded distinctly uncomfortable, his gaze shifting from her to the man at her side. 'We weren't expecting you this weekend, Brett.'

'A change of plan.' The other's tone was level enough, but with an underlying note that drew Lisa's somewhat puzzled glance. 'I understand we acquired a masseuse?'

The discomfiture increased. 'It was your idea to bring in a resident.'

'You found it necessary to go all the way to England to find someone?'

'Well, no. I just happened to need treatment while I was over there, and Lisa here came across as exactly the right person for the job. The best technique I've ever known!'

'I'm sorry.' Lisa was looking from one to the other in growing perplexity. 'I seem to be missing something.'

Gary's face registered sudden comprehension. 'I thought you knew,' he said. 'Brett—Mr Sanderson owns the Royale.'

CHAPTER TWO

LISA'S immediate impulse as she met the steady grey eyes was to lash out, verbally at least. He had made a total fool of her, and deliberately so. It took a real effort to speak with cool composure.

'Why didn't you tell me who you were?'

'I didn't consider it necessary,' he said. 'You were due to find out soon enough.'

'So am I to understand that I don't have a job after all?'

The broad shoulders lifted in a brief shrug. 'Seeing you're already here, that will depend on whether you can justify my manager's faith in you. Three weeks should be long enough to judge, but we'll allow six for good measure. Neither of us has had breakfast yet,' he added to the manager. 'Miss Renshaw might appreciate hers in her room. I'll take mine in the restaurant.'

He moved away, tall, lean and in command. Lisa watched him go with a heavy heart. Of all the people in the world she might have met on the way here, it had to be her ultimate employer! Considering the circumstances, she supposed she should be grateful that he hadn't thrown her straight out on her ear.

'I'm sorry,' proffered Gary Conway on a rueful note. 'I'd hoped to have you up and running and already proving your worth before Brett arrived. As I said, it was his idea to have a resident masseur in the first place.'

'But not all the way from England, and definitely not a woman.' Lisa forced a lighter note, determined not to take it out on the man facing her. 'At least I have six weeks.'

'More, if you prove as popular with the clientele as I'm sure you will. Brett's a hard-headed businessman, but he's also keen on customer satisfaction. The Royale has a reputation second to none in providing it.' He added curiously, 'How did the two of you meet up, anyway?'

'On the plane coming over from San Juan.' Lisa saw no reason to mention the previous meeting. 'I thought he was simply being courteous when he offered me a lift. I'm surprised that a man of his standing wouldn't have private air transport to and from the island.'

'He'd normally use the company jet all the way through,' Gary confirmed. 'He was still in Boston Friday evening, so he must have flown down to San Juan yesterday.'

'A summons he couldn't resist, perhaps?' Lisa suggested with irony, recalling the way he had been dressed the previous evening. 'I imagine he has women friends most places.'

Gary laughed. 'You could be right. I can think of a couple over there who might be worth making the trip for—although he'd have had to leave uncommonly early this morning to make the shuttle over here.' His shrug dismissed the subject. 'Anyway, I'll have someone show you where you'll be living. You can tell Room Service what you'd like for breakfast.'

'I'm not all that hungry right now,' she said truthfully. 'I can wait till lunchtime.'

'Your choice, of course, although Room Service is twenty-four hour if you change your mind. Come on back across after you've unpacked, and I'll show you around.' He gave her a reassuring smile. 'Don't worry. Everything will be fine.'

Lisa hoped he was right. The last few minutes had rubbed a great deal of the shine off her expectations. There were several questions she wanted to ask, but this wasn't the time. Gary had his own concerns. Later, they could perhaps re-establish the friendly accord they had known back home. She wasn't attracted to him in any romantic sense, nor he to her, she was sure, but they had certainly got along.

One of the bell-boys was detailed to show her to her quarters and carry her bags. He did so cheerfully, leading the way out through the rear of the lobby and down a tree-lined path to a separate, two-storeyed building. Spanish-style archways opened on to a covered terrace running the whole way round the upper floor, with the rooms below shaded by the overhang. Bougainvillaea spilled in vibrant contrast across the white stone.

Lisa's room proved to be on the upper floor. Surprisingly spacious, and well-furnished, it had floor-length windows which opened on to the terrace, with privacy assured by the drapes and reed blinds. The floor was tiled in pale beige, with one or two bright rugs scattered around, the bed hidden inside a comfortably padded sofa set within an alcove created by flanking and overhead cupboards. A small but perfectly adequate shower-room and toilet completed the appointments.

All the staff quarters were like this, advised the young bell-boy, whose name was Cleveland, although most of the staff came in on a daily basis.

'Mr Sanderson very good employer,' he declared in lilting West Indian accents. 'Though he not always here. Mr Conway a good man too,' he added judiciously. He gave her one of the flashing friendly grins she found so appealing, and left her to it.

Unpacked, and with the morning still comparatively young, Lisa took a few minutes out on the terrace. From this angle it was possible to see only a small part of the harbour, with the open sea beyond stretching to the distant line of the horizon. Another large ship was on its way in. Apparently St Thomas was a major port of call on most Caribbean cruises.

The ships added to rather than detracted from the general scene, though the numbers of tourists who disembarked must make the town itself very crowded. St Thomas was a free port, with all the shopping attractions signified by that classification. Not all that much use, of course, to the average English visitor, considering the limited duty-free allowances on return to the country, Lisa acknowledged. She would have to watch her own purchases while she was here.

She was beginning to get over the disheartenment. It was going to be up to her to show Brett Sanderson her capabilities. Gary had mentioned speaking to him in Boston, which it seemed might be his main base. He probably wouldn't even be around for the greater part of her six-week trial.

It was coming up to ten o'clock when she made her way back to the lobby. Gary was already there, talking with a couple of guests. Lisa made sure he had seen her, then parked herself unobtrusively by a potted palm to wait until he was free, content to watch the comings and goings.

Some of these expensively clad men and women would be clients of hers in the near future. Cosmetic customers for the greater part, wanting nothing more than a relaxing, oil-scented session on the treatment table beneath pampering hands, but strained muscles were commonplace too among vacationers. Lisa was happy to provide either service. It was all part and parcel of the job.

'Sorry about that,' said Gary, breaking away at last and coming over. 'Two of our regular guests. They've spent the whole of November here every year since we opened.'

'That must have cost a small fortune,' commented Lisa lightly.

'More a medium-sized one. Isle Royale doesn't come cheap. I thought we'd start with your working premises. We run a small gymnasium for the keep-fit enthusiasts. The room you'll be using as a salon is just off it. Some prefer privacy in their own apartments, of course.'

The gymnasium was situated in the basement of the hotel, but, because of the lie of the land, not wholly below ground. The outside wall had been replaced by glass sliding doors giving access to the gardens. From there a path meandered down to a spacious sun deck surrounding a free-form pool, both at present well-populated. The view, as from all points of this place, was outstanding. Lisa thought she would never tire of looking at it.

Well-equipped for its size, the gymnasium had only one client at the moment—a man in his fifties who might well be *her* first client, the way he was straining to lift those weights, Lisa judged.

'There really should be someone around to supervise,' she said diffidently, approving the layout and general appearance of the treatment-room next door. 'Left to themselves, people often overdo things.'

'The gym's supposed to be closed on a Sunday,' Gary admitted. 'The cleaners must have left the door unlocked.

If he's still there when we go, I'll ease him out.' He ran an eye over the neat white tunic she was wearing. 'You don't need to dress in any uniform, by the way. You'll probably find shorts and a T-shirt far more comfortable.'

The pristine tunic dress, complete with name-badge, had been *de rigueur* at the London salon. Lisa had donned it automatically, along with the white shoes that went with it. Shorts and T-shirt might suit the climate, but she would feel less than professional in them. The treatment-room was air-conditioned anyway.

Gary spent the next half-hour showing her over the whole hotel. He even took her up to one of the superlative private suites, at present unoccupied, although guests were due, he said, the next day.

'Full house,' he added with satisfaction. 'And the same right through to New Year. You'll enjoy a Caribbean Christmas.'

With brilliant sunlight pouring through the windows, and a temperature outside in the eighties, it was difficult to accept that Christmas was a mere four weeks away, Lisa reflected. It would be her first non-family event, but her parents were appreciative of her career priorities. If things didn't go too well, she would be home again anyway early in the new year.

Think positively, she told herself firmly at that point. If she did fail to make a go of it, it wasn't going to be for want of trying.

Curved around a corner of the building, the suite's balcony offered an expansive view of the grounds and surrounding landscape in addition to the harbour and sea. Lisa followed the line of steps leading from a side-patio to a split-level dwelling further up the hillside, though still within Royale territory.

'That's Brett's place,' said Gary. 'He lives mostly in Boston, but this is where he likes to relax.'

'I don't imagine he gets the chance too often?' she said hopefully.

'Occasional weekends, longer breaks as and when he can fit them in. Sunday's an odd day for him to arrive, hence the surprise. He usually comes down for a week or so over Christmas, which is another reason why I didn't expect to see him now. Not that he couldn't retire here permanently if he wanted to.'

Was there an element of envy in that latter remark? Lisa wondered, slanting a swift glance at Gary. Having a boss who was not only rolling in wealth but ten years younger to boot couldn't be an easy pill to swallow.

'Either a workaholic, or just plain greedy,' she commented lightly. 'It takes all sorts.'

Gary shrugged. 'Brett's OK. He mostly leaves me to run the Royale the way I see fit.'

'Except in this one instance?'

'That's understandable too, I guess. I acted on impulse. He wouldn't consider that a businesslike approach.'

'Are you regretting having brought me out?' she asked.

He smiled then and shook his head, gaze dwelling for a moment on the curve of her mouth. 'No way.'

The sudden flicker of doubt was swiftly dispatched. She was reading too much into too little, Lisa told herself.

'I'd better be getting back downstairs,' he said. 'If anything is scheduled to go wrong, you can bet it will happen when I'm out of the office. I've had a notice mounted on the board, so you might find yourself in demand already. No appointments before Tuesday, though. You'll need tomorrow to get over jet-lag.'

So far she wasn't experiencing any, Lisa reflected, going down in the lift. The stop-over in San Juan might have helped.

Noon here was five o'clock in the afternoon back in England. Last Sunday at this time she had been saying goodbye to her parents before returning to London to finish out her notice at the salon. With the family home as close as Northwood, she had visited them often, so they were all going to feel the deprivation—especially if the job did become permanent. Independence had its drawbacks.

Not that she regretted stepping out on her own, lonely though she sometimes found herself with her two flatmates both involved in serious relationships. Boyfriends came and went, but there was no one she felt anything deeply about. This job offer had opened up a prospect for a new life all round. She wasn't about to let it slip through her fingers without an almighty struggle.

'I'd prefer to eat with the other staff,' she said when Gary suggested that she join him in the restaurant for lunch in an hour's time. 'I don't expect any special privileges.'

'Just today, then,' he insisted. 'Call it a welcoming gesture.'

Lisa capitulated with some reluctance. Hobnobbing with management on her very first day was hardly likely to get her off on the right foot with the rest of the staff. Gary should be aware of that. He had gone far enough already in choosing to show her round the place himself.

She went back to her room and exchanged the white tunic for a simple shirtwaister dress in cream and green striped cotton, the shoes for strappy sandals. The three sun-bed sessions she had allowed herself these past couple of weeks had renewed her summer tan to a point where she felt confident enough to go bare-legged. It was so good to be free of tights again. They'd certainly never be needed in this climate.

A stroll around the grounds and the hotel, at her own pace, took up most of the rest of the morning. Most of the guests she saw appeared to be middle-aged or older, with just one or two younger couples and no sign at all of children. Not the kind of place for a family holiday, Lisa conceded, though nice for a honeymoon, perhaps, providing one was far enough up the income ladder.

A series of resonant blasts signified the imminent departure of one of the cruise ships. She would have liked to watch it pull out from the wharf, but it was already five to one, and time to meet Gary Conway in the restaurant.

The latter was at the front of the hotel. Mr Conway was already seated, the *maître d'* informed her when she presented herself. He led the way, an imposing figure of a man in his dark blue jacket and pale blue trousers, threading his bulk with dexterity between well-populated tables and more tropical greenery out on to a shaded apron terrace where several more tables were set.

Lisa's steps faltered when she saw Brett Sanderson seated with Gary, but it was too late now to back out because he had seen her. Both men rose politely to their feet as the *maître d'* pulled out a chair for her, making her feel even more discomfited. There was no reading anything from Brett Sanderson's expression, but he could hardly be delighted to have her thrust on him again so soon.

'I didn't realise you'd be here too, Mr Sanderson,' she said a little stiffly as she took her place.

The grey eyes remained unrevealing. 'I like to mingle on occasion. You're all settled in, I take it?'

'More or less.' She could think of nothing to add to that statement. That gaze of his was so penetrating. She felt like a microbe under a microscope!

Gary came to her rescue, handing across a leather-bound menu, his smile easy. 'Take your time. There's a lot of choice. Would you like a drink to be going on with?'

'I'm quite happy with the iced water,' she said as a waiter appeared at her elbow to pour a brimming glass.

'Dieting?' asked Brett Sanderson.

She gave him a level look. 'No.'

'That makes a change. Most women are obsessive about it.'

'The ones you know, perhaps. I've never had a weight problem myself.'

'The ones *I* know don't either,' came the dry return, 'but it doesn't seem to make any difference. There's little joy in taking a woman out to dinner when all she does is pick at her food.'

'Perhaps you make them nervous,' Lisa suggested with deliberation.

A glint sprang in his eyes. 'Do I make you nervous?'

'Not enough to put me off my food. Especially,' she tagged on, 'when it's as good as I'm sure the Royale provides. Of course, I don't anticipate eating in the restaurant every day.'

'The staff have choices from the same menu,' came the steady reply. 'You won't be losing out.'

Lisa flushed a little, aware of being put in her place. She had asked for it, of course. Brett Sanderson wasn't a man to allow innuendo of that kind to pass. If she wanted to stay out at least the six weeks, she couldn't afford to indulge the antipathy he aroused in her.

The arrival of another waiter to take their order smoothed over the awkward moment. With no prices shown on the menu, Lisa opted for what she hoped was one of the least expensive starters and main dishes.

This was luxury living with a capital L, she thought, sitting back in her seat to view the seascape visible over Gary Conway's shoulder while they waited for the food to arrive. The sunlight danced on the water, turning the surface silver. A solitary yacht moved slowly across her line of vision, sails whiter than white against the blue backcloth of the sky.

'You'll need transport to get around,' said Brett Sanderson, startling her because she had thought him involved in business matters with Gary. 'You can drive?'

'Yes,' she acknowledged. 'But——'

'There's a spare jeep you can use, if you don't mind a bit of a rough ride.'

'That's very...thoughtful of you,' she said, not about to look this particular gift horse in the mouth. 'I'd certainly like to get to know something of the island while I'm here.'

'So you said earlier. You'll need a map. The road system isn't extensive, but neither is it all that well signposted. Magen's Bay is only over the hill, if you fancy a day at the beach when you're free. It's one of the ten finest in the world, according to *National Geographic*.'

'Sounds great.' Lisa wondered why he was being so congenial all of a sudden—unless it was to make up for his initial attitude. 'Thank you.'

Brief though it was, his smile quickened her pulse-rate. 'You're welcome.'

'Lisa has a brother in the hotel business,' advised Gary. 'Trainee chef at the Savoy, no less!'

'Impressive. We should bear him in mind for future reference.'

Sensing patronisation, she said coolly, 'I doubt if he'd be interested. His sights are already set.'

'Then we'll leave him be, of course.'

Lisa bit her lip, this time aware of derision. She had been too quick to jump; the remark hadn't been meant to be taken seriously. Brett Sanderson had her in a state of flux, hardly knowing *how* to take him. She had a feeling that he was deliberately playing with her.

The meal progressed pleasantly enough. The food, Lisa found, was superb, the service unhurried, though no less efficient for it. She felt uncomfortable being treated as a guest by their waiter, and tried to convey as much, but the man's face remained impassive, relaxing only when his employer asked after his wife and family.

'Loxley's been with us a long time,' said Gary over coffee. 'As have many of the staff. A job at the Royale carries a lot of prestige.'

'It also carries a higher rate of pay than average,' put in his superior drily. 'Loyalty doesn't come free.'

'I doubt if it can be bought either.' Lisa steeled herself against the regard swung her way. 'Not the genuine kind, anyway.'

'The genuine kind,' came the reply, 'is a luxury few can afford. Take yourself as a case in point. If you're as good as Gary says you are, then your previous employers must have been loath to lose you, but your loyalty to them didn't last long when matched against a better offer.' He shook his head as she made to speak. 'I'm not criticising, just underlining.'

Lisa held her tongue. There was little enough she could say in the circumstances to refute that line of reasoning. Yes, she had been implored to stay on at the salon, and yes, she had found Gary's offer too good to resist. Who wouldn't have? Brett Sanderson might be an out-and-out cynic, but he was probably right in this instance. Genuine loyalty sometimes called for more self-sacrifice than most people were prepared to entertain.

'Which particular method of massage do you favour, by the way?' he asked unexpectedly, jerking her out of her thoughts.

'It depends on the client,' she said. 'Swedish for those I sense are looking for stimulation rather than relaxation, more along Eselan lines otherwise. I'm also studying reflexology.'

If she had hoped to blind him with science she was to be disappointed.

'That's foot massage, isn't it?'

'It can be applied to the hands too, although the feet tend to give a clearer indication.'

Gary was looking a trifle puzzled. 'Indication of what exactly?'

'There are reflex connections in the feet which link to the rest of the body,' Lisa explained. 'So any problem will show up as a sore spot on the foot, then the complaint can be treated by massaging the corresponding part of the body.'

'Sounds a bit speculative,' came the doubtful comment.

'It isn't,' she assured him, well accustomed to the same reaction. 'I'm still in the process of learning, so I can't claim total expertise, but it really does work.'

'I don't have any problems that I know of,' said Brett, 'but I think it might be an idea if I sample your technique for myself before turning you loose on my clientele. Shall we say three o'clock?'

It was more in the nature of an order than a suggestion, and one she was in no position to refuse, Lisa conceded, reluctant though she was to be put through her paces this way.

'Of course,' she said with what composure she could muster. 'You're entitled to know what you're getting for your money.'

The grey eyes held a hint of mockery. 'Every time.'

He finished his coffee, then pushed back his chair to get to his feet, waving Gary down as the latter made to rise with him.

'Relax. I'm going up to the house. See you in an hour,' he added to Lisa.

'Less, actually,' she returned with purpose. 'It's already ten past two.'

'So it is.' The mockery increased. 'Fifty minutes, then, and counting, if we're going for split-second timing.'

That was what she got for being so darned pedantic, she told herself ruefully as he moved away. Meeting Gary's eyes across the table, she gave a wry smile. 'I don't think I've made much of an impression up to now.'

'He can't fail to be impressed by your technique,' he assured her. 'And that's what matters most. The trouble is, he's too used to having women fall over themselves to please him.'

Lisa didn't doubt it. With his looks, position and money, Brett Sanderson could have just about any woman he wanted—and probably did. Who was it who said that familiarity bred contempt?

Gary was called away as soon as they left the restaurant. In this job, he said without rancour, there was no such thing as a regular day off.

Back in her room, Lisa put on the suggested shorts and T-shirt, took a look at herself in the mirror and discarded both items to don the white tunic again. Regardless of what Gary might think, she felt far more comfortable this way. She had a feeling too that Brett Sanderson might not be quite so liberal in his views on what constituted suitable working apparel where she was concerned.

Cut to curve smoothly inwards just below chin level, her hair was long enough to fasten back or even up when she felt the need of a change. A shorter style might suit the climate better, but she was loath to have it cut—especially while there was any doubt at all about the length of her stay. She could be as positive as she liked about it, but where Brett Sanderson was concerned nothing was certain.

One thing she did know: there would be no boot-licking on her part. If she did retain the job it would be purely on merit.

Although it was still only half-past two, she made her way down to the health club. The doors were now locked, but Gary had supplied her with a key.

The treatment-room was beautifully cool and airy, the cupboards well-stocked. She chose a cinnamon-based oil as the most likely to suit the man in question, and made sure the table padding was secure, the top sheet fresh and clean. After that it was simply a case of waiting for her employer to arrive.

He appeared on the hour, wearing shorts and T-shirt himself, legs long, well-muscled and deeply bronzed. Lisa steeled herself to show no reaction when he emerged from the changing-room with nothing but a towel wrapped about lean hips. His was by no means the first male body she had worked on—although it was certainly one of the finest, she was bound to admit.

'If you'd like to make yourself comfortable on the table...?' she said in what she hoped was a suitably neutral tone.

He did so, lying face down with arms stretched out in an attitude totally lacking in self-consciousness. Lisa laid the back of her hand lightly against the hollow of his back to form the first contact while she poured a little oil into her cupped palm, feeling the slight but unmistakable tensing of muscle at her touch and experiencing an involuntary and unprecedented response she found hard to ignore.

She began with the slow, smooth stroking motion that was the first level of massage, allowing her senses to become attuned to the contours and textures of the powerful shoulders and tapering back. The muscle was well-defined while lacking the ugly over-development so many men moved mountains to attain, the whole structure honed to a fine edge of fitness that left no single ounce of surplus flesh. A body any masseur would find pleasure in, thought Lisa, forgetting her former hostility as she gradually broadened and deepened the pressure.

He made neither sound nor movement as she worked, but lay there in total relaxation, dark head turned to one side, eyes closed. His mouth in repose lost none of its firmness. An uncompromisingly masculine face in its strong boning, yet not a hardened one, Lisa reflected. As Gary had made no mention of a wife, she assumed he was unmarried—although it didn't necessarily follow that he had never been married, of course. Divorce was all too common these days.

He wouldn't be an easy man to live with, for sure. His kind would expect to rule the roost. There were women prepared to go along with that arrangement, she supposed, but it certainly wouldn't suit her!

A matter hardly likely to concern her, anyway, came the semi-humorous rider. Brett Sanderson was way outside her league.

The more intensive pressure of level-three massage brought the occasional faint grunt from his lips, but he made no demur. Lisa repeated the whole process down each leg, finishing off with a lightly flowing stroke over the full length of his body.

'Would you like to turn over now?' she said with rather less detachment than she would have liked. 'That's assuming you want the complete half-hour treatment?'

He made no verbal response, but simply did as she suggested, a slight twist to his lips as he gazed up at her. His chest was broad and deep, with a dark curl of hair tapering down between the pectorals. The towel had slipped low enough to expose the ridging of muscle across his abdomen, bringing a sudden dryness to Lisa's throat and an undeniable fluttering of her own stomach muscles.

'You obviously exercise on a regular basis,' she heard herself saying.

'Whenever I can,' he confirmed. 'I have a home gym back in Boston.'

'That's where your other business interests are?' Lisa bit her lip in recognition of the obvious, seeing the ironic expression in the grey eyes. 'Another hotel?' she hazarded.

He shook his head. 'The Royale was strictly a one-off.'

'But a highly successful one.'

'You could say that.' He lifted a quizzical eyebrow. 'Do we continue?'

'Yes, of course.' Lisa could feel the warmth under her skin, and only hoped it didn't show. For the first time in her working life she was reluctant to carry on with a treatment—self-conscious beneath that mocking gaze of his. He knew it too.

She poured more oil into her palm, willing herself to calmness as she began work on shoulders and upper arms, avoiding any direct eye-to-eye contact. It wasn't easy because he never shifted his gaze from her face, but she persevered, unable, though, to do anything to stop the churning sensation in her stomach. So much for professional objectivity, she thought wryly. She was reacting like some total beginner!

Whatever her inner responses, her hands retained their skill, moving with supple dexterity from one level to another. This time she used knuckles as well as fingers and thumbs in the final stage, going deeper than was absolutely necessary in deliberate if not exactly ethical retaliation for the discomfiture he was causing her.

His sudden move to grasp her by the nape of her neck and bring her head down to his took her so much by surprise that she had no chance to take evasive action. His mouth was ruthless in its heady demand, sending vibrant tremors down the whole length of her spine. As kisses went it didn't last long, but while it did it was devastating.

'Payment in kind,' he said, letting go of her. 'I think we might call the session over.' He came upright, lips tilting sardonically as she took an involuntary step back away from him. 'Never been kissed before?'

'I'm not accustomed to having clients take that kind of advantage,' returned Lisa frostily, recovering some degree of poise. 'Or do you consider your position gives you special privileges where your female staff is concerned?'

'On the assumption that they might value their jobs too much to complain?' He sounded distinctly amused. 'It's a thought I hadn't considered. Not that it applies here anyway.' He paused, eyeing her speculatively. 'Are you in the habit of inflicting pain on those you take a dislike to?'

Lisa felt her cheeks warm again. She made an effort to regain control of the situation. 'If I went too deep for comfort, I'm sorry. It certainly wasn't intentional.'

'Yes, it was.' The tone was unequivocal. 'You were aching to pay me back for not declaring myself from the outset.'

Guilt sharpened her tone beyond the bounds of discretion. 'Don't be ridiculous!'

A glint sprang in the grey eyes. 'Don't *you* be insubordinate. Whatever the circumstances, I do happen to be your employer. Try showing a little respect.'

Lisa clamped down hard on the instinctive reply. If he was deliberately trying to rile her into telling him what he could do with his job, he wasn't going to succeed. She had come a long way for it, and intended making a go of it, no matter what drawbacks there might be.

'That's better,' he said when she remained silent. 'It's a wise woman who knows when to hold her tongue.' He slid off the table, repositioning the towel without undue haste when it threatened to slip even further. 'I can find no fault with your general technique, but we'll have to see how it goes down with the clientele. In my experience, most women prefer a masseur to a masseuse, although I've no doubt you'll attract more male customers than usual. If you have any trouble with any of them, I'll want to know about it.'

'If I do, I can handle it myself,' she returned stonily, and received a derisive glance.

'The same way you handled it a few minutes ago? I said I want to know. Clear?'

He didn't wait for an answer. Lisa drew in a long, slow breath as he disappeared into the changing-room, fighting the urge to put her fingers to her still tingling lips. Brett Sanderson had to be just about the most infuriating man she had ever met, but there was no denying the physical effect he had on her.

No problem, she reassured herself. He wouldn't be asking for any further treatment. As to his latter instructions, if the situation he had been speaking of should arise, she would use her own judgement.

CHAPTER THREE

WITH several appointment requests already received via Guest Services by the Sunday evening, Lisa dispensed with the advised day's rest. The jet-lag hadn't materialised, and she was here to work, not laze around. There would be time enough for island exploration later.

Gary was delighted with the interest engendered, and even more so by the reports filtered back to him of client satisfaction with the new addition to the staff over those first few days.

'You've already vindicated my trust in you,' he enthused on the Friday afternoon when she dropped by his office in response to his request. 'I knew you wouldn't let me down.' He sat back in his chair to regard her with unconcealed admiration. 'You look as fresh as a daisy! Don't you ever get tired?'

Lisa laughed. 'I'm working no harder here than I did back home—and in far superior surroundings.'

'Surroundings you haven't left as yet, I'm told.'

'Plenty of time for that over the weekend.' She added tentatively, 'Does that offer of the use of a car still hold good, do you know?'

Gary looked surprised. 'Why wouldn't it?'

'No particular reason,' she prevaricated. 'Just that I thought Mr Sanderson might have forgotten making it.'

'I shouldn't imagine so for a moment, but if you're in any doubt at all, why not confirm with him? He just got in.'

'I didn't even realise he'd been away again,' she said.

41

'He went back to Boston Tuesday morning. Unusual for him to make another trip down so soon, but it's his time. I've been pretty tied up myself these past few days,' he tagged on, 'but I'll be free tomorrow with any luck. I'd be delighted to take you on a tour of the island.'

Lisa had been looking forward to discovering the place on her own, but it would be churlish, she reflected, to say so. Gary was putting himself out for her; she could do no less for him. She smiled and nodded.

'Thanks.'

'My pleasure. Why don't we have dinner together to-night too?'

Lisa eyed him for a brief moment of uncertainty before deciding to take the bull squarely by the horns. 'It's nice of you to ask me, but I don't think it's a good thing that we be seen spending too much time together, do you? Some people might get the wrong idea.'

His brows drew together. 'Such as what?'

'Such as the suspicion that my coming here was rather more than just a business arrangement. You and I know it's not true, of course, but that's how it could look. I've a feeling Mr Sanderson would see it that way, at least.'

Something close to chagrin flickered briefly in the eyes opposite, then he smiled and shrugged. 'Maybe you're right. In which case, we should maybe forget about the island tour too for the time being.'

'It might be best.' Lisa greeted the ringing of the telephone with an inner relief. 'I'll leave you to it. I've another appointment in fifteen minutes.'

She made her escape without haste, still not all that certain that she hadn't been barking up the wrong tree. But, even if that was so, what she had said still made good sense. Any suspicion at all on Brett Sanderson's

part that her and Gary's relationship was in any shape
or form of a personal nature and she would be out of
here for certain.

At the very least she was now free to spend her leisure
time the way she wanted, although the question of the
car still remained. The hotel ran a twice-daily shuttle to
and from town, and taxis were in ready supply if one
was prepared to pay the price, but transport of her own
was obviously the most convenient. She could, she supposed, always hire a car. The only real need would be
at the weekends, so the cost shouldn't be too prohibitive.

Her next appointment was the last of both the day
and the week. Not a new client; Lisa had already treated
the man twice before. He had suffered a strained shoulder
muscle in the pool on the Monday, and was still experiencing some stiffness in the area. Like some others,
he preferred to receive treatment in the privacy of his
own suite.

With the king-size beds both too low and too wide for
such usage, it was the practice for staff to set up a spare
treatment table in the suite itself when required. She
found her client already laid out on it when she arrived.

He had stripped only to the waist as treatment was
confined to the area of the injury. Apart from the
sprinkling of grey in the mid-brown hair, and a certain
lessening of skin elasticity, Richard Hanson showed little
enough sign of his fifty-odd years. A widower for the
last five of them, and obviously wealthy enough to do
as he liked, he spent his winters in the Caribbean, moving
from island to island as the fancy took him, his summers
back home in Boston where he had a married son he
didn't get along with all that well.

Lisa was well-accustomed to being on the receiving end of such confidences. In Richard's case, she sensed a certain loneliness beneath the urbane exterior, and wondered why he hadn't remarried. It could hardly be for lack of opportunity.

'I think this session should do the trick,' she said as she worked on the damaged muscle. 'When will you be moving on?'

'I'm not sure,' he said. 'I might stay on over Christmas again after all.'

The hotel was fully booked right through to New Year, Lisa recalled Gary telling her, but no doubt someone of Richard Hanson's ilk would be accommodated should he decide to extend his stay. There was a small though equally luxurious annexe to cater for any possible overflow.

'I hear Christmas at the Royale is something special,' she commented.

'Yes, it is. In fact, I've found few hotels to compare with this place at any time. Brett Sanderson cuts no corners.'

'You know him on a personal level?'

'Only through coming down here on a regular basis, though he runs one of the city's major companies back home. We're both in property development. Leastways we were, before I decided to take an early retirement and enjoy life. If he's any sense, he'll do the same when he hits the fifty mark. There's no point in carrying on for the sake of it. Especially when he has this place to come back to.'

'Some people find it difficult to fill their time without work,' remarked Lisa mildly. She brought the arm back and up, gently stretching the tendon. 'Does that pain you at all?'

'No, it feels just fine.'

'In which case, I think we'll call it a day. If there's any recurrence, you can always come back.'

'I'll do that.' He sat up, easing the shoulder a little gingerly as if still not wholly convinced of the cure, and then with growing confidence. 'You have a wonderful touch!'

'Glad to be of help,' she said lightly. 'Just be careful not to overdo it in the pool for a while.'

'I will.' He slid off the table and reached for the shirt he had thrown over a nearby chair, watching her as she folded the white sheet and padded underlay into a neat stack. 'What do you do with your off-duty time?' he asked unexpectedly.

'I haven't had any yet,' Lisa acknowledged. 'But I've a whole lot of sightseeing to do.'

'I'm invited to a party tomorrow evening,' he said, 'but I don't have anyone to take. Would you consider taking pity on an old man yourself?'

Lisa gave him a swift glance, saw the smile and had to laugh. 'Older, perhaps—hardly old!'

'Would you consider partnering an older man, then?' He held up a staying hand as she made to speak, recognising the refusal trembling on her lips. 'No ulterior motives, I promise. All I want is someone I can feel comfortable with.'

'There must be plenty of those,' she said. 'What about that woman you were talking with on the patio this morning?'

'The woman who was talking to me, you mean. She's on the look-out for a new husband.'

'And you don't fancy being it?'

'I don't fancy *her*. A hard piece if ever I saw one!' There was humour in the last comment. 'Anyway, I'm not looking for another wife.' He paused, assessing her hesitation. 'At least think about it, will you?'

She should give him a firm negative here and now, Lisa knew, but she couldn't somehow bring herself to do it. 'No ulterior motives', he had said, and she believed him. All he wanted was companionship. She could surely provide that.

The words were out before she had properly decided. 'All right, I'll come. Where is this party?'

'The other side of the island. Magen's Bay.'

'Island people?'

'Not in any real sense. The Gordons are from Boston too. They use the house as a year-round retreat for any family members able to take advantage of it. The daughter, Andrea, comes down regularly. She's a great party-thrower, and not so very much older than you are yourself, so you won't find the guest list confined to people of my age-group.'

'You don't need to sell me any further,' Lisa assured him, casting aside any remaining doubts. 'I already said yes. About what time would you want to go?'

'Nine.' He added softly, 'And thank you for trusting me, Lisa.'

'No big risk,' she returned on a bland note. 'I've been taking karate lessons for over a year.'

His laugh was unforced. 'A sensible move this day and age. I'll see you at nine, then, out front.'

It would be rather nice to have somewhere in particular to go on her first Saturday evening, Lisa conceded as she left the suite. Tomorrow, too, she must phone home again to let them all know how things were going. Postcards and letters were a good back-up, but they took far too long to reach their destination.

One of the duty receptionists called her as she crossed the lobby. 'Mr Sanderson wants to see you,' he said. 'You're to go up to the house.'

A summons that intimated trouble of some kind, thought Lisa with more than a little trepidation, although she couldn't for the life of her think what she might have done to merit any complaint. Sunday's little episode was still too clear in her mind to allow for insouciance of any kind where Brett Sanderson was concerned. The man was unpredictable.

The temptation to slip back to her room and change out of the white tunic first was quickly and firmly squashed. She wasn't out to create any impression but that of efficiency at her job. She refused even to glance in a mirror to check her appearance.

Built to the lie of the hillside, the house itself was on more than one level, with the uppermost fronted by a spacious patio containing an oval swimming-pool. Reaching the top of the steps at last, Lisa stood for a moment to gather her breath while taking in a view surpassing even that to be seen from the hotel.

With sunset no more than half an hour away, the horizons were already tinged with pink and gold against the blue, the island outlines deepened, the whole scene so achingly beautiful that it brought a lump to the throat. She wished her family could only be here with her to see it too. It didn't seem fair that she alone should be so fortunate.

'Having trouble?' asked an all too familiar voice, and she turned abruptly to see Brett Sanderson standing a few feet away. He was wearing rope-soled espadrilles along with the white drill trousers and casual navy blue shirt, she noted fleetingly, which explained why she hadn't heard him approaching. His expression gave no hint of what his mood might be.

'It's quite a climb,' she said.

'Good exercise. There's a road comes in round the back for those who find it too much for them.' He indicated the table and chairs set out under a blue and yellow striped umbrella on the far side of the pool. 'Come and have a seat. I'll fetch us a drink. What would you like?'

'Fresh orange juice, if you have it, please,' she said a little disconcertedly.

He smiled briefly. 'On American territory there's *always* fresh orange juice. The same goes for ice. The sun's over the yard arm, so how about making a Buck's Fizz of it?'

Lisa shook her head. 'Champagne doesn't agree with me, but do go ahead yourself.'

'I'll stick to whisky,' he said. 'Five minutes.'

She watched him make his way inside via sliding glass doors before moving, rounding the pool to take one of the cushioned chairs as instructed. Whatever it was he had to say to her, it couldn't be so bad or his manner would surely be very different. All the same, she found it impossible to relax.

He was back well within the five minutes, carrying a tray with a whole jug of iced orange juice, along with a small whisky decanter and glasses. There was also a dish each of nuts and crisps—or chips, as they were known here.

'Saves making another trip,' he said, depositing the tray on the table. 'Help yourself.'

'Don't you have any help in the house?' Lisa ventured as he took a seat.

'I don't do the cleaning, if that's what you mean,' came the dry return, 'but I've no desire for full-time service.'

'With the Royale so close, I don't suppose you need it. You can always phone through for anything you want.'

'One of the advantages of living on the doorstep, so to speak, yes.' He poured himself a whisky, lifted the glass to her in brief salute. 'So how have you found your first week?'

Not quite a week as yet, it was on the tip of her tongue to answer, but she held it back, recalling the last time she had indulged in pedantry. 'So far so good,' she said instead. 'Unless you've gained a different impression?'

'On the contrary, I've heard nothing but praise. Even the women you've treated seem pretty impressed with your technique.'

'Why the "even"?' she demanded. 'What difference does it make?'

His shrug was easy. 'Most women prefer a man's attentions. It's called human nature.'

'I'd call it typical male generalisation!' Lisa retorted scathingly, forgetting who she was talking to for the moment. 'We're not all the same!'

'You reach flashpoint fast!' he observed without a change of tone. 'Ever tried counting to ten before you let fly?'

She bit her lip, aware that he had a valid point. Her temper had always been hot, her tongue liable to run away with her. A habit it was more than time she learned to control.

'I apologise,' she said.

'Lip-service.' He was giving no quarter. 'But we'll let it pass—this time.' He watched her face, accurately judging the struggle going on inside her, if his somewhat

sardonic smile was anything to go by. 'Is it just me who
rubs you up the wrong way, or are you always this
prickly?'

'I already apologised,' she said, side-stepping the
question. 'It won't happen again—sir.'

The grey eyes took on a warning gleam. 'I admire spirit
in a woman, but don't press your luck too far.'

Her temper flared again, kept from expressing itself
only by the suspicion that he was deliberately piling on
the pressure. Why she wasn't sure. If he wanted an excuse
to send her packing, she had already given him enough
ammunition. In any case, he had pronounced himself
satisfied with reports so far.

'Am I still on six weeks' trial?' she asked with purpose.
'Or did you decide I was good enough at my job to bear
out Gary's faith in me?'

'It's early days yet,' he said. 'We'll see out the six
weeks.' He paused. 'Speaking of Gary, I trust the association is strictly business?'

'Of course.' She did her best not to over-emphasise.
'What else would it be?'

'You're a very attractive young woman, and he took
on a whole lot of work in obtaining the necessary
permits—to say nothing of the risk he ran.'

'Meaning he might have lost his job?'

'Meaning I might have lost faith in his judgement. He
isn't usually given to snap decisions in any sphere. Hiring
you on the strength of a couple of salon sessions was
hardly what I'd call good policy.'

'He took rather more than that into consideration,'
answered Lisa shortly. 'My training, the salon's reputation, for example. The question of personal involvement never entered into it.'

'Good.' There was no hint of apology in his tone.

'I take it you already faced Gary with the same question?' she said. 'Wasn't his answer good enough?'

'Let's just say I didn't find it entirely convincing. Anyway, enough of that. Relax and enjoy your drink. The sun's about to set.'

Lisa would have preferred to leave while she was still on top of her warring instincts, but she could hardly just walk out. She picked up her glass and sat back in her chair, concentrating her attention on the golden orb already lowering behind the rim of hills on the furthest island.

Within mere seconds it had slipped completely from sight, leaving the multi-hued, cloudless sky to merge by slow degrees into one great glowing orange canopy. Flat calm, the sea was tinged the colour of beaten copper.

Lights began twinkling as dusk spread its wings, the traffic moving along the waterfront far below like twin strings of glow worms. The cruise ships still in dock were outlined by strings of coloured bulbs from bow to stern. As if at a given signal, the cicadas started up, filling the air with their vibrant tune.

Lisa drew in a deep breath, temporarily oblivious of the man seated opposite. Every sunset here was different, every evening an experience to be savoured.

'Not the best, but good enough,' commented Brett, bringing her down to earth again. 'Did you ever get to see the green flash?'

'What's that?' she asked.

'A phenomenon that sometimes occurs at the very moment that the sun disappears. It's supposed to bring good luck to those who do see it.'

'Have you?'

'No.' His smile was brief. 'I'm willing to believe those who swear they have, but I doubt if it's caused by any-

thing other than atmospheric conditions. We make our
own luck—good *or* bad.'

'You can't *make* a non-tangible substance,' she said
with deliberation. 'That's a contradiction in terms.'

Surprisingly, he failed to rise to the provocation. 'Attract, then. Whichever, it isn't written in the stars.'

Lisa didn't agree, but wasn't about to say so. Lights
had come on along the front of the house and round the
edge of the pool. Automatic timers, or light-sensitive
power cells, she assumed. The water looked inviting.
Tomorrow, she promised herself, she would find a beach
and take her first swim.

'The car you spoke of,' she said before she could lose
heart. 'Is it still available?'

'Certainly. I left instructions with the bell-captain to
let you have the keys whenever you were ready. All you
have to do is ask him.'

'It's very good of you.'

'Isn't it, though.' The irony was back in his voice.
'More orange juice?'

She shook her head again, drained what was left in
her glass and put it back on the table before getting to
her feet. 'I'll leave you to enjoy your evening,' she said
formally. 'And thank you again for the car.'

He had risen to his feet along with her, his expression
difficult to define. 'Remember it's left-hand side here,
like England. You might find it awkward at first with
left-hand drive too, but that's the way it is. You can pick
up an island map in the lobby.'

'I already did,' Lisa acknowledged. 'I've been studying
it all week, so I shouldn't have too much trouble finding
my way around.'

She could feel his eyes on her back as she made her
way across to the steps. They were well-lit, so presented

no difficulty in the descent, but she found her legs oddly shaky as she did so. Half an hour with Brett Sanderson was enough to put anyone on edge, she told herself. He was anything but a relaxing presence.

It was more than just that, she knew. Dislike him though she might, she was also strongly attracted to the man. It all stemmed from that kiss the other day. It had been more in the nature of reprisal on his part, but it had woken something in her that wasn't easy to put aside. The less she saw of him from now on, the better for her peace of mind.

She ate dinner at eight, chatted for a while with one or two other members of staff, then took a walk around the grounds before retiring to her room to write up her diary for the day. She had kept a diary since she was fifteen, and had every one of them stored back home, although she had never, so far, got round to re-reading any of them.

Tonight she made no more than a passing reference to the Royale's proprietor, but described the sunset in detail. There had been, and would be again, others even lovelier, but this was the one she knew she would remember in years to come.

Awakening next morning to the sound of pouring rain, she thought for a moment that she was back in England. By the time she was showered and dressed, however, the cloud had passed over and the sun was shining again, the foliage no longer dripping.

Fresh water—or the shortage of it—was a major problem here in the islands. Most buildings were constructed so that run-off from the roof was piped directly into holding tanks, but drinking water came in bottles. Lisa found it difficult always to remember not to fill her tooth mug from the tap, although she had suffered no ill-effects so far from her occasional lapses.

The bell-captain handed over the keys to the jeep without comment when she approached him, but there was something in his expression that made her wonder how many others of the staff had ever been offered the same privilege. She neither expected nor wanted to be singled out for special treatment, yet that was how it must look.

Too late to hand the keys back now, she decided. The damage was done. She could, however, limit the effect by just using the jeep this one weekend, and sorting out her own transport after that.

She found the vehicle easy enough to handle, if a little deficient in creature comforts. There was a canvas body shell over the front two seats but the rear end was open to the elements, allowing a welcome through-draught in lieu of air-conditioning. As Brett had warned her, it felt distinctly odd to be driving on the left-hand side of the road in a left-hand-drive car.

With just the two cruise ships in at present, now seemed as good a time as any to take a look round the town, leaving the afternoon free for more extensive exploration, and perhaps the promised bathe before returning to the Royale. She would need to be back no later than eight-fifteen to leave herself time to prepare for the evening's outing, Lisa reckoned. She was quite looking forward to this party.

Descending the hill, she narrowly avoided running into the back of the vehicle ahead when it pulled up without warning in order for the driver to pass the time of day with another man walking at the roadside, neither showing the least concern at the near-miss. A not uncommon occurrence, she found, when the same thing happened again bare minutes later. Reflexes here needed to be razor-sharp.

She was fortunate enough to find a vacant space in a car park just off the waterfront. It was a lot hotter down here, and noisier too. Taxis cruised the streets touting for custom, the drivers seemingly taking it for granted that any pedestrian was looking for transport back to the ships. Almost every other shop on the crowded Main Street appeared to be a jewellers, windows ablaze with gold and precious stones on offer at incredible discounts. Given free choice, Lisa wouldn't have known which way to turn.

She was gazing at a display of diamond earrings in one window when she sensed someone looking over her shoulder.

'If you're thinking of buying,' said Brett Sanderson, 'don't bother with this stuff. It's strictly tourist fodder.'

Lisa forced a laugh. 'The price would still be over my head. In any case, I'm hardly likely to buy myself diamonds, whatever the quality.'

'No,' he agreed. 'It should be up to the man in your life to supply that kind of thing.'

'Hardly likely.' She made herself turn, looking up a long way to meet the grey eyes and regretting the lack of heels to bring her more in line. The thonged sandals were comfortable for walking and driving, but added little in the way of stature. 'I wouldn't have expected to see you down here,' she added lamely.

'Normally, you wouldn't have,' he admitted. 'Not at this hour. I have to see someone. How did you find the jeep?'

'Fine.' She hesitated, not sure this was the right time yet reluctant to let the opportunity pass. 'I'm grateful, of course, but perhaps it might be a better idea if I find my own transport after this weekend.'

Dark brows lifted. 'Why would you want to do that?'

'Because I think it might be resented by other staff. Being English puts me in an awkward enough position to start with.'

'On the premise that my being English born too might suggest some closer relationship?'

'I didn't mean that.' She was hard put to it to maintain any composure. 'It has to be obvious that we're not...'

'Involved in an affair?' he supplied sardonically as she searched for the right words. 'We've been alone together on two quite lengthy occasions, neither of which will have gone unnoted. I dare say the fire is already fuelled.'

'If you really thought that, why send for me to come up to the house last night?' she demanded, abandoning restraint. 'You could have said all you had to say in the office.'

His shrug was dismissive. 'I prefer an informal atmosphere. It's up to you whether you use the car or not, of course, although I'd think turning it in now might cause even more speculation. Anyway, I have to get going, so have a nice day.'

He gave her a mocking salute, and moved off, leaving her standing there looking after him with knitted brows. It was ridiculous, of course. No one could possibly believe there was anything between them. He had simply been making fun of her.

She spent the following hour or so exploring the wealth of narrow, shop-lined alleys running from Main Street through to the waterfront, ate a casual lunch at one of the cafés on Hibiscus, and made her way back to the car around one o'clock to find herself hemmed in by one of the open-sided buses used to transport tourists about the island.

With no sign of the driver in the vicinity, Lisa had no recourse but to sit it out until he put in an appearance some twenty minutes later. He'd been for lunch, he said cheerfully when she pointed out her dilemma. He'd shift the bus right this minute.

It was actually another ten minutes before he finally did so, due to an exchange of repartee with a taxi driver who pulled up on the street. By the time she did manage to get into motion again, Lisa had acquired a whole new philosophy. Where was the rush, anyway? She had all day.

CHAPTER FOUR

IT WAS gone seven and fully dark when Lisa finally returned to the Royale after a day of bright yellow sunshine, white-pink beaches and limpid turquoise seas. She had swum from Limetree in a water temperature of around eighty degrees, and watched iguanas in the palm trees while lazing on a lounger and sipping iced fruit juice from the beach bar. Altogether an idyllic end to the week.

Her next-door neighbour was a girl her own age who was employed on Reception. Selina Destry had been among the first to offer a friendly hand. She was just coming off duty when Lisa arrived back.

'If you've nothing planned for tonight, I'm meeting up with some people down town in an hour or so,' she offered casually as they climbed the stairs together. 'You'd be welcome to join us.'

'I'd have liked that,' said Lisa regretfully, 'but I already have an arrangement. Perhaps we could make it another time?'

'Sure.' Eyes bright with curiosity, she added, 'Anybody we know?'

It was obvious who she meant, underlining Brett's earlier words. Lisa set out to scotch any conjecture in that direction.

'I'm going to a party with Richard Hanson—suite 113.'

'Oh?' Selina sounded taken aback. 'How did you manage that?'

'He needed someone to take, and asked me, that's all.'

'He's twice your age,' said the other girl judiciously. 'You know what folk are going to think?'

Lisa kept her tone light and even. 'Only those with nothing better to think about.' They had reached her door. 'Thanks for asking me, anyway.'

Selina took the hint, shaking her head in resignation. 'See you,' she said.

With the door closed, Lisa stood for a moment to consider the situation. Any kind of association between an older man and a younger woman was liable to misinterpretation, perhaps, but was she prepared to be governed by what some people might see fit to believe? Richard Hanson simply wasn't that kind of man. She could trust her own judgement on that score.

She chose to wear a softly draped silk jersey skirt and matching wrap-over top in a pale cream that enhanced her tan. With her simple gold chain and earrings, she looked neither over- nor under-dressed, she judged, viewing herself in the mirror. Now that the time was near, she had to confess to a certain nervousness concerning this party. Apart from Richard, she would be among total strangers—and she didn't even know him all that well.

They were all just people, she reassured herself. She had never found any difficulty in fitting in before, so why should now be any different?

Richard's reaction when he saw her was a reassurance in itself. 'You look just perfect!' he claimed extravagantly. 'Such class!'

'You didn't expect me to turn up in jeans and T-shirt, did you?' asked Lisa demurely, and he laughed.

'If I'd thought that might happen I wouldn't have asked you in the first place. You strike me as a very well-balanced and mature young woman.'

Which just went to show how wrong impressions could be, she reflected humorously.

Richard had ordered a taxi for the journey. He preferred to be driven, he acknowledged on the way. Especially on vacation.

'I'm determined not to stagnate in retirement like so many before me,' he said. 'There are a lot of places I never had time to visit—a whole lot of experiences to catch up on. I've been snorkelling for the first time this last week. Wonderful!'

'Something I've yet to try myself,' Lisa confessed. 'I'm not all that strong a swimmer, so I've tended to cry off in the past.'

'With fins, and providing you don't try it on your own, you don't need to be strong swimmer,' he assured her. 'I went out with a party on the yacht Brett makes available to hotel guests. You'll have to come too next time.'

'I'm only free at the weekends,' she said. 'At least, I hope to be kept busy all week.'

'I don't think there's any doubt about that. You've already established a reputation. It was an excellent idea all round to bring in a full-time masseur—or masseuse in your case. Brett should be congratulated.'

'I wasn't his choice,' Lisa admitted. 'Gary Conway gave me the job. I have six weeks to prove myself.'

'You already did, my dear.' Richard was comfortingly confident. 'I'll make sure Brett knows it.'

'I'd as soon let my performance speak for itself,' she said. 'But thanks, anyway.'

By night the huge and lovely horseshoe of Magen's Bay lacked much of its visual attraction, though the sweeping crescent of beach far below shone white in the moonlight when they crested the winding road. Halfway down the hill, they turned on to a narrow lane culminating in a large square courtyard where many cars were already parked.

Judging by the sounds issuing from the white-walled house, the party was already into its stride. Lisa trod gingerly across the expanse of gravel in her flimsy sandals. Scraped heels would hardly enhance her image at a time when she was going to need every ounce of self-confidence.

From a central hall, wide arches opened on to several rooms all thronged with people. Lisa gained an immediate impression of superb décor and the kind of luxury she was beginning to equate with St Thomas— so far as the wealthier inhabitants were concerned, at any rate. She had seen enough of the island today to appreciate the demarcation lines between the rich and not so rich, although there seemed to be no real poverty here either.

'We'll find a drink and then mingle,' said Richard. 'Supper won't be on before eleven at the earliest, so I hope you're not too hungry as yet.'

With food the last thing on her mind at the moment, Lisa murmured a suitable response. At least Richard knew people. That had to make things easier. All she had to do was relax and be herself.

Mingle they did over the following hour or so. Introductions were on a casual, first-name basis, with newcomers to a group drawn immediately into whatever topic of conversation happened to be in force at the time. Much of the talk was of a semi-gossipy nature involving island affairs, but Lisa was happy enough to listen and learn.

Separated from Richard at one point when he went to refill their glasses, she found herself close by one of the sliding glass doors leading out to a jutting terrace, and slipped through on impulse to get some fresh air for a minute or two.

The night was balmy, the sky devoid of cloud, the stars so bright it hurt to look at them. Leaning on the stone balustrade, Lisa gazed out over the spangled seascape and thought how fortunate she was to have this opportunity. It was a different world out here, a totally different way of life. Not that she would want simply to idle the days away as some of people she had met tonight appeared to do.

'I thought it was you I spotted a while back,' said a heart-jerkingly familiar voice behind her, and she straightened abruptly as the owner of it moved up to her side.

'You seem to make a habit of this,' she said.

Brett Sanderson lifted his irritatingly mobile left eyebrow. 'Habit of what?'

'Coming up on people unexpectedly.'

'Pure circumstance,' he declared. 'I usually seem to catch you in deep contemplation of something or other.' He leaned on an elbow, half turned towards her. 'I didn't realise you were acquainted with anyone here.'

Lisa refused to acknowledge any disquiet. 'I came with Richard Hanson. He's probably looking for me. He only went to fetch drinks.'

The dark brows had drawn together. 'Hanson?'

'Suite 113,' she confirmed. 'He was short of a partner to bring.'

'And you were more than willing to fill the breach, of course.' Brett came upright again, all trace of good humour vanished. 'He's old enough to be your father, for God's sake!'

The anger was all-consuming. 'He's also a thorough gentleman,' she snapped. 'Which is more than can be said for someone who thinks the way you're obviously thinking!'

'You can take it from me that everyone who's seen the two of you together tonight will be thinking the same thing,' came the hard retort. 'And with good reason. When a girl your age takes up with a man of Hanson's age there's usually one binding factor, and that's money. If catching yourself a millionaire was the idea when you persuaded Gary into offering you a job, you lost little time in sorting out the wheat from the chaff!'

Lisa drew in a sharp breath. 'Point number one, I did *not* persuade Gary to give me a job,' she denied with heat. 'If that's what he's intimated, then he's a liar! It happened exactly the way I told you. He was injured and I treated him.'

'To a promise he couldn't resist?' The tone was cutting. 'I can't condone his falling for it, though I can to a certain extent understand it. You're a tempting prospect for any man.'

'How very flattering.' Lisa's tone was honey-sweet, her better judgement swamped by pure fury at the insult. 'Do you include yourself in that assessment, Mr Sanderson?'

His mouth took on a derisive slant. 'I believe I already answered that question the other day. Not quite what you were looking for, though, was I?'

'You're talking through your hat,' retorted Lisa scathingly. 'I don't have to listen to this!'

He reached out and caught her by the wrist in a grip of iron as she began turning away, dragging her back round to face him. 'You'll listen! After tonight you don't see Richard Hanson on a social level again. Not while you're working for me!'

'I wasn't aware of any ruling against staff-guest friendships,' she said with deliberation.

'I just introduced one. And you'd better take heed of it.'

'You'll be telling Richard that too?' she asked. 'I'm sure he's going to be absolutely delighted to hear your opinion of his ethics!'

'It's *your* ethics I'm concerned with,' came the short, sharp answer. 'If you're not prepared to stay away from him, you can start packing.'

She regarded him with loathing. 'Do you act the overlord in your private life too, or is that reserved for your underlings?'

Grey eyes sparked and the hand on her wrist tightened still further, yanking her to him. His other arm slid around her lower back as he bent his head to find her mouth with his in a long kiss, bringing her up hard against him and holding her there. Lisa felt her senses swimming, the drumming of blood in her ears. She staggered when he put her away from him at last.

'I treat as I find,' he said between his teeth. 'And I don't make threats lightly.'

'And I don't take that kind of treatment lightly!' It was all Lisa could do to keep her voice from cracking. 'If I fetch Richard out here now, you might like to tell him to his face what you believe my motives to be, and see what he thinks. Of course, it's very possible that he'll take offence at the realisation that you consider him stupid enough to be taken in by a gold-digger, but why should you care about *his* feelings? After all, he's only a paying guest.'

Brett eyed her narrowly. 'That comes close to blackmail.'

'I'd call it closer to tactical strategy.' Lisa was past caring what impression she might be creating. 'It's your choice—*Mr* Sanderson.'

It was evident from the tautening of his jaw that the delicate emphasis did not go unnoted. For a brief moment he looked dangerously close to grabbing hold of her again. Lisa took an involuntary step back, halting any further retreat through sheer effort of will as she saw his lip start to curl.

'It might be a good idea if you went back inside,' he said, 'before I lose sight of the main object altogether.'

She stood irresolute for a second or two before giving way, reluctant to allow him the last word on the subject. When she did turn away it was in mute recognition of the futility in any further exchange. He wasn't going to believe her, no matter how many times she denied the charge. She had killed any hope of that herself.

Richard was talking with a small group not far from the door when she got inside. He spotted her at once, beckoning her over with a smile.

'I was beginning to think you'd gone back to the Royale,' he said.

From somewhere Lisa dredged up a smile of her own. 'I went out to look at the view.'

'Not really the best time to see it,' declared the tall and striking brunette standing next to him with an air of authority. 'Sorry to have been so long in doing the rounds, but it's quite a crowd. I'm Andrea Gordon.'

Lisa tried her best to sound suitably buoyant. 'You have a lovely home, Andrea.'

'Thank you.' From her tone it was obvious that the compliment meant little. 'Richard was telling me you're a qualified masseuse.'

'That's right.' Lisa added with deliberation, 'Employed at the Royale.'

The amber eyes took on a new expression. 'Oh, really?'

'English too,' commented one of the other women in the group with interest. 'Brett must have gone to a lot of trouble to find you.'

'I was hired by Gary Conway,' returned Lisa clearly. 'I consider myself very lucky to be here.'

'Lisa underrates herself,' said Richard. 'She's worked wonders on my strained shoulder. You should give her a try, Felicity.'

'I might just do that,' agreed the latter.

'I'm not sure I'd be allowed to treat non-residents,' put in Lisa hastily. 'I've been kept very busy this past week.'

'Hardly surprising if you're as good as Richard says you are,' came the unperturbed response. 'I'll have a word with Brett.'

'You can do that right now.' Andrea was looking in the direction of the doors through which Lisa had come, a faint frown creasing her forehead. She lifted a hand. 'Brett! Over here a moment, darling!'

Lisa froze inside as he joined the group. Dressed, as most of the other men were, in a well-cut lounge suit, he looked completely at ease. His glance passed over her as if they had never even met, the smile turned on purely for Andrea herself.

'Felicity has a request to make,' she said.

'Fire away,' he invited the older woman, who looked not in the least put out by being put on the spot that way.

'I'd like to have Lisa here give me a treatment, if that's OK,' she said. 'Richard was telling us how good she is.'

Brett's expression remained impassive. 'If she can fit you in, by all means—providing you pay the set fee.'

Felicity laughed. 'As if I'd expect special rates!' To Lisa herself, she added, 'I'll give you a call tomorrow and arrange a time.'

'Fine.' Lisa took care not to look at Brett. Apparently her threat to bring Richard in on the accusation he had made had been enough to make him think twice about taking the matter any further. In this instance at least. Whether he would be prepared to leave it at that remained to be seen. Whichever, she vowed fiercely, she wasn't going to be browbeaten into submission. He had gone too far!

The group dispersed, the members moving on to merge with other groups. Lisa went where Richard led, playing the party girl to the best of her ability. Occasionally and unavoidably, they crossed paths with Brett, but he gave no indication of what he might be thinking. All the same, Lisa doubted if she had heard the last of it.

So just let him try to get rid of her on this pretext! she vowed. She would fight tooth and nail if necessary to keep this job.

They were well into the small hours before people began leaving. Hardly liking to be the one to suggest a retreat themselves, Lisa was highly relieved when Richard finally made the move.

Andrea was talking with Brett when the two of them went to make their farewells; an intimate conversation, Lisa conjectured, seeing the tantalising little smile on the other girl's lips, the proprietorial manner in which her hand rested on his sleeve. Brett was smiling too, his whole attitude that of a man quite happy to be appropriated. Andrea was welcome to him, Lisa thought sourly. Any attraction she herself might have felt was long flown.

She took her leave of their hostess with creditable composure, winged a brief, 'Goodnight,' in Brett's direction, and accompanied Richard from the house to the taxi summoned by telephone.

'You didn't find it all too boring, I hope,' he said a little anxiously as they moved off down the drive. 'Some of the permanent residents do tend towards insularity.'

'I found it all very entertaining,' Lisa assured him. 'They seem a very friendly crowd.'

'For the most part,' he agreed. 'You're not in any trouble with Brett Sanderson, are you?' he added unexpectedly.

Lisa forced herself to stay cool. 'Why should you think that?'

'Just something in the way you looked when you came in from the terrace. You *were* with him out there?'

Considering the fact that he had followed her in bare moments later, she could hardly deny it, thought Lisa wryly. Aloud, she said, 'Well, yes, but there was no trouble.'

'Good. It crossed my mind that I might have put you in a difficult position. Some hotels have strict demarcation rules where staff and guests are concerned. I must confess, it never occurred to me to ask.'

'If there had been any I would have told you.'

'Yes, of course you would.' He patted her hand. 'I've very much enjoyed your company tonight, Lisa. Would you be prepared to spend an evening with me again?'

Had it not been for Brett's intervention, she might have considered more carefully before answering, 'I'd like that too.'

Richard looked gratified. 'Better still, how about visiting St John with me tomorrow? It's no more than twenty minutes by ferry. It's very beautiful and quiet over there. More than half of it is a National Park, so there's little commercialisation.'

Once again rancour outweighed better judgement. Her smile was light and bright. 'It sounds idyllic.'

'That's settled, then.' He leaned forward to address their driver. 'We'll need transport to Red Hook for the nine o'clock ferry.'

'Sure thing,' agreed the man cheerfully.

The Royale's lobby was quiet when they went in, with only the night clerk to witness their parting. Richard made no attempt to prolong the moment, thanking her once more for her company and leaving her to make her way out through the rear of the main building to the staff quarters.

Only when she was in her room with nothing to do but prepare for bed did Lisa begin to question the wisdom of her actions. No matter how innocuous the relationship, did she really want to spend a whole day with a man old enough, as Brett had pointed out, to be her father? Richard was nice, and obviously lonely, but there were several women closer to his own age here at the Royale on their own too—and not all of them, she was sure, out to trap a new husband.

While it was a little too late to call tomorrow off, she would accept no further invitations, she resolved. The fact that by doing so she would appear to be obeying Brett Sanderson's instructions was by the way. The decision was entirely her own.

That resolve weakened considerably over the course of the day, however, for the simple reason that she had rarely enjoyed herself as much. Richard proved himself the perfect companion—an interesting conversationalist with a dry sense of humour, undemanding yet innovative too. It was his suggestion that they hire a couple of scooters to tour the island after exploring the tiny harbour town with its nameless streets and laid-back atmosphere.

Time seemed almost to stand still here, Lisa found. The islanders themselves moved through life at a leisurely pace that paid little heed to the passing of the hours. She had thought St Thomas beautiful, but St John surpassed it in sheer scenic charm.

They avoided the famous Trunk Bay where hundreds of cruise-ship passengers were likely to flock, and settled for a near-deserted little beach backed by waving palms on which to eat the lunch of bread and cheese and fruit they had purchased at the incongruously modern Mongoose Junction shopping centre back in Cruz Bay.

'We should have brought bathing things,' Richard observed with regret, looking at the gently lapping, so invitingly blue water a few yards away.

Lying back on the sand, hands clasped beneath her head, eyes closed against the sun, Lisa murmured a lazy response. Simple though the food had been, it had tasted so good out here in the unsullied air. She felt replete, happy to while away an hour just being.

She must have dozed off, because when she opened her eyes again Richard was no longer within sight. Sitting up, she saw him standing down at the water's edge, hands thrust into the pockets of his shorts.

A fine figure of a man for his age, she reflected, watching him pick up a pebble and skim it over the surface. He should marry again. He was too young to spend the rest of his life on his own.

As if sensing her eyes on him, he turned back to look at her, a smile creasing his lips when he saw she was awake.

'Sorry,' Lisa offered ruefully as he came up. 'I don't usually fall asleep in the middle of the day.'

'A mixture of climate and late nights, I expect,' he said. 'I was halfway there myself.' He paused, eyeing her with a certain speculation. 'Brett Sanderson seems to have made quite an impression on you, one way or another.'

She gazed back at him with drawn brows, pulse suddenly erratic. 'What makes you say that?'

'You were saying his name in your sleep.' His eyes crinkled at the expression on her face. 'Don't look so horrified. It *was* just his name.'

'I must have been having a bad dream,' she claimed. 'I detest the man!'

'Oh?' He sounded intrigued. 'Would it be too inquisitive of me to ask why?'

Lisa forced a shrug, a lighter tone. 'It's just the way he is, I suppose. He expects automatic compliance with his every word!'

'While you object to being told what to do?'

'When it's my own business, yes.'

Richard studied her thoughtfully for a moment. 'Something did happen between the two of you last night, didn't it?' he said. 'Was it anything to do with me, by any chance?'

Lisa bit her lip. Short of an outright lie, she had backed herself into a corner.

'If it was, I think I have a right to know,' he insisted gently.

'He thinks I'm after your money,' she admitted with reluctance.

'And are you?'

She looked up with furious words of denial trembling on her lips, saw the twinkle in his eyes and subsided again on the realisation that she was being teased.

'It isn't funny,' she said. 'He won't be the only one thinking that way.'

'But it didn't stop you coming out with me again today.'

Picking up a handful of sand, she allowed it to trickle through her fingers, avoiding his gaze. 'As I said, I object to being told what I can or can't do. Not that I dislike being with you,' she added hastily. 'You're very good company, Richard.'

'On a strictly platonic understanding.' He held up a hand as she made to speak, his smile reassuring. 'I had a twenty-year-old daughter killed by a drunk driver three years ago. We were very close, and you remind me very much of her. That's why I want to spend time with you.'

'I'm so sorry.' Lisa scarcely knew what else to say. 'What was her name?'

'Helen.' His tone was reminiscent. 'Her hair was the same colour as yours. She could sit on it when she was younger, but she had it cut to shoulder-length when she started law school——' He broke off, shaking his head. 'Enough of that. If it's going to cause you any problems, I'll stay away from you, of course.'

'There's no need,' she assured him decisively. 'I'll be very happy to spend time with you, Richard. You said something about snorkelling?'

'Yes, I did.' He looked and sounded fortified. 'If you're sure, I'll make arrangements for next weekend. And perhaps you'll have dinner with me one evening before then?'

'Love to,' she said, and meant it. So far as she was concerned, Brett Sanderson could go take a hike.

They spent what was left of the afternoon looking round the ruins of a former sugar plantation high up on a point above another picturesque bay, ate a leisurely supper under the stars at a little restaurant called Back Yard, and caught the last ferry back to St Thomas by the skin of their teeth.

It was almost ten o'clock when they reached the Royale—early by most standards, but Lisa for one was ready for a good night's rest.

'It's been simply great!' she told Richard. 'I've enjoyed every minute!' On impulse, she reached up and pressed a swift kiss to his cheek. 'Goodnight, and thank you again.'

Selina was on duty at the desk. 'Mr Sanderson's been asking for you,' she said as Lisa went past on her way to the rear door. 'You're to go up to the house.'

Not at this hour, thought Lisa flatly, acknowledging the message with a smile and a wave of her hand. Whatever he had to say could wait until morning. Richard would straighten things out for her if she asked him to, she knew, but why should he? Their relationship was nothing to do with anyone else but the two of them.

She was in bed though not yet asleep when the telephone rang. Something Richard forgot to say, she surmised, lifting the receiver. It was a shock to hear Brett Sanderson's voice on the line.

'You were to come up to the house when you got in. Why didn't you?'

'Because it's late, and I have an eight-thirty appointment in the morning.' Lisa could hardly believe her own control. 'If you're going to tell me to pack my bags——'

His laugh stunned her into silence. 'I guess I did go over the top some,' he said. 'No excuses; I was out of line.' He paused, seemingly waiting for some response from her. 'Apology accepted?' he asked at length.

She found her voice again with an effort. 'Is this some kind of joke?'

'Hardly. I'm trying to straighten things out between us.'

'Why?' The word came out jerky.

'I'd have thought that obvious.'

'Not to me.'

It was a second or two before he spoke again. When he did it was on a softer note. 'You must know I'm attracted to you, Lisa. Thinking about you with Hanson——'

'It isn't the way you think,' she interjected, still unable to believe he was serious but unwilling to miss the opportunity of putting things right. 'I remind him of his daughter, that's all. The one who was killed three years ago.'

'I didn't know about that. I don't know *him* all that well, when it comes right down to it.' His voice briskened. 'So, we'll leave him aside. Have dinner with me tomorrow night, then *we* can start getting to know one another better.'

Lisa hardly knew what to say—hardly knew what she felt. 'I don't think——' she began.

'Then don't think,' he said. 'Just act. Eight o'clock here at the house. I'll be waiting.'

He had rung off before she could find any response. Replacing the receiver, she collapsed back on the pillows to gaze at the shadowed ceiling with confused emotions. From last night's anger to this was too much to take in all at once. If Brett really was attracted to her—and why would he tell her so if he wasn't?—then what exactly had he in mind so far as getting to know one another better went?

She wasn't going to find out, she told herself firmly. Whatever Brett Sanderson's plans might be, she was playing no part in them.

CHAPTER FIVE

MONDAY was a busy day, with little time to think of anything very much apart from work. Preparing for her final client of the afternoon, Lisa was surprised to see Gary Conway walk in.

'I understand you've been spending a lot of time with Richard Hanson,' he said without preamble. 'I don't think it advisable for staff and guests to become personally involved.'

'We're not——' she began, but he shook his head.

'I'm just pointing out hotel policy. Brett wouldn't go for it.'

'He already knows about it,' Lisa answered coolly. 'He was at the party Richard took me to on Saturday night. He said nothing about hotel policy.'

Gary looked nonplussed for a moment, then rallied to say with force, 'He doesn't have to contend with staff discipline the way I do. If I pass this up I'm opening the way for other liaisons. Our guest services may be second to none, but we're not running an escort agency!'

'Perhaps you'd better ask Brett what he thinks before you start laying down the law,' she suggested, and added, giving way to a spurt of anger, 'Or perhaps I could mention it for you. I'm having dinner with him tonight.'

That took the wind completely out of Gary's sails. He gazed at her in obvious confusion. 'Since when?'

Already regretting the too hasty retort, Lisa sought refuge in brevity. 'Since he asked me. I've another client due in a few minutes, so can we leave it at that for now?'

76

'I may have been right about your professional abilities,' he snapped, 'but I certainly had you pegged wrong otherwise! You're a real smooth operator! Just don't run away with the idea that Brett might prove a better proposition than Hanson, if it's a long-term arrangement you're looking for. He doesn't go in for them.'

He was gone before she could come up with a reply, leaving her wryly aware that Brett might have been right in suspecting his manager's motives where she was concerned. Looking back on that week of their meeting back home, she could think of no time at which she might have given the impression that she was interested in the man as much as the job he was offering. True, she had taken him home and introduced him to her parents, but only in order to reassure them that she wasn't about to be whisked away by some adventurer.

However the misunderstanding had arisen, he wasn't entirely to be blamed for thinking her an opportunist. She had contributed to that impression herself by tossing Brett Sanderson's name in his face the way she had. Her temper again. One of these days she would learn to think before she spoke.

Explanations would be a waste of time, she decided ruefully. All she could do was let it ride. The way things were going, there was every chance that she wouldn't even be seeing out the six weeks.

Despite the previous night's resolution, she found herself in two minds as eight o'clock approached. While she wanted neither long- nor short-term association with the Royale's owner on any personal basis, she could hardly just leave him sitting up there waiting for her to join him either. A phone call declining the invitation was the obvious answer, but she had left it a bit late even for that.

The only civil way, she concluded, was to go and keep the appointment, but in a manner that left him in no doubt of her lack of interest in furthering the association. Unaccustomed as he undoubtedly was to having a woman turn him down, he would probably find it difficult to believe, but believe it he must.

Wearing black crêpe evening trousers along with a white silk shirt, she made her way up to the house via the steps at eight o'clock on the dot, hoping no one had spotted her. Brett greeted her on the patio, where a table had been laid for two, complete with tall green candles in silver candelabra and a beautifully arranged centrepiece of local orchids.

'I thought you might prefer to eat outside,' he said. 'There's so little opportunity for alfresco dining in England. What will you have to drink—other than orange juice, that is?'

'I'd love a piña colada,' Lisa returned with purpose. 'Richard introduced me to them yesterday.'

There was no visible reaction in the grey eyes. 'Piña colada it is. Make yourself comfortable.'

She took a seat on the canopied swing sofa, breathing in the night scents and listening to the ceaseless strumming of the cicadas. Staying totally detached from a man who could make her heart thud this way with just a look was clearly out of the question. The best she could do was try not to let it show.

By the time Brett returned with the drinks she was in command of herself—on the outside at least. He had forsworn whisky in favour of a piña colada himself, topping each glass with slices of fresh pineapple.

'To a better understanding,' he toasted.

Of what? Lisa wondered, concentrating on her glass as he took a seat at her side. She was supremely aware of his nearness—of the muscular length of his thigh beneath the fine cream linen of his trousers. His shirt was dark brown, the hand-stitched tailoring emphasising his breadth of shoulder by the very act of defining it.

'I was half expecting you not to turn up,' he said.

'What would you have done if I hadn't?' she asked, and sensed his smile.

'Come to find you, of course.'

'In other words, no one is allowed to say no to Brett Sanderson.'

'Only if they say it loud and clear and at the proper time. If you're still smarting over the other night,' he added, 'why not get it out of your system?'

'I already did,' she said. 'Loud and clear and at the proper time.'

His laugh held genuine amusement. '*Touché*! So we start afresh.'

'With what in mind?'

If anything the amusement increased. 'What do you think I might have in mind?'

'It's supposed to be a feminine prerogative to answer a question with another,' Lisa stalled.

'True enough, but I'm still asking.'

She nerved herself to be direct. 'All right, so I'm wondering why you should have changed your whole attitude towards me so suddenly. Saturday night, you accused me of having an eye to the main chance.'

'I already apologised for that. If you'd explained the situation then it wouldn't have got that far in the first place.' He paused, eyeing her with a speculative expression. 'Why didn't you?'

'Because I didn't consider it your business,' she returned levelly. 'I'm entitled to choose my own company for my own reasons, without having to answer to anyone else.'

'Even when that anyone else happens to be your employer?'

'You have no jurisdiction over my free time.'

'But I apparently have enough pulling power to fetch you up here.' Brett's tone was light, but his eyes challenged her to deny it.

'I came,' she said, 'because you gave me little opportunity to refuse.'

'You could have rung any time today.'

'I've been too busy to think about it.'

'Of course.' It was obvious that he didn't believe a word of it. 'You're proving very popular. Just don't overdo things. Those who don't get seen today get seen tomorrow.'

'I know my limitations,' she said coolly.

'In other words, you'll do as you see fit.'

'If that's the way you want to take it.'

Brett gave a somewhat exasperated sigh. 'If you're trying to provoke me, you're heading in the right direction.'

'I'm not trying to provoke anything,' she denied. 'Just don't "little woman" me, that's all. I can handle my own business affairs.'

He was silent for a long moment, studying her thoughtfully. 'You really don't like me very much, do you?' he said, startling her with the directness of the comment. Did liking have anything to do with the way he made her feel? she wondered fleetingly.

'To be perfectly honest about it,' she heard herself answering, 'no, I don't.'

'Why exactly?'

The tension he created in her was building to a point where it had to find some release. Eyes sparkling like twin sapphires, she gave it to him straight.

'Your arrogance for one thing. You think you only have to crook your little finger to have everyone falling over themselves to please you! Well, I'm no yes-woman either.'

His smile was ironic. 'I'd never have guessed it. Don't stop there. Tell me more.'

Lisa took a hold on herself. 'Why bother?' she said shortly. 'I'm obviously not making any impression.'

'Oh, but you are. You did the very first time I set eyes on you.' He ran the tip of a finger lightly along the length of her forearm, sending a *frisson* down her spine. 'You'd just been through an experience that would leave most women too shaken up to have any spirit left, but you bounced right back. I remember the way your eyes flashed at me when I suggested it might have been reckless taking that walk on your own. I had a powerful urge to kiss you right there in the street!'

Lisa was silent, not at all sure that he wasn't making fun of her. When she did find her voice it sounded surprisingly steady. 'It's perhaps as well you didn't give way to it, or I might have thought I'd jumped out of the frying-pan into the fire!'

'You might indeed.' Brett was watching her face, his expression devoid now of mockery. 'I'm feeling the same urge right this moment. You have a mouth made for kissing.'

'Not on an empty stomach,' she said lightly, registering the implied promise too late.

He took the remark at face value—or appeared to do so. 'Then we'd better eat.'

Taking her still more than half-full glass from her, he deposited it along with his own on the low table in front of them, then pressed a bell set into the surface and got to his feet, stretching out a hand to her. 'Come on.'

Lisa allowed him to draw her upright and lead her across to the ready-laid table, sliding into the chair he pulled out for her with a feeling that her grip on events was already beginning to slide. Like him or not, she was drawn to him, but trusting him was another matter entirely. It was going to be essential to keep a clear head.

The man who came out from the house pushing a loaded trolley was instantly recognisable to her as one of the restaurant staff. That he recognised her too was apparent from his expression, although he covered the surprise quickly enough. Lisa sat self-consciously while he served the pair of them with beautifully arranged platters of fresh seafood, thankful when he left them to it and retired indoors again.

'You realise that it will be all round the hotel by morning?' she said.

Broad shoulders lifted. 'I expect it will.'

'Don't you care?'

He regarded her quizzically. 'Do you?'

'I have to live and work down there.'

'Your reputation is likely to suffer far more from your association with Richard Hanson,' he pointed out, 'but that doesn't appear to concern you too much.'

'That's different.'

'I agree. He's twenty years older than I am, to start with.'

'There's nothing between us.' Lisa tried not to overdo the emphasis. 'I already explained his interest in me.'

'And I believe you. Those not in the know will continue to think the same way I thought initially.'

'And still thought when you phoned me last night,' she said with deliberation.

The strong mouth slanted. 'A matter of priorities. To get back to what we were talking about, people being the way they are, it's nigh on impossible to maintain a totally unsullied image. If you were really so concerned with outside opinion yourself, you wouldn't be here at all.' His tone lightened. 'How do you like the conch?'

Lisa accepted the change of subject without demur, aware that she had made the same point herself only last night: one couldn't live one's life in constant fear of what others might think. On the other hand, there was such a thing as deliberately laying oneself open to misinterpretation. Her having dinner tête-à-tête with the Royale's owner after one short week here was unlikely to be viewed with anything but cynicism.

She hardly needed to ask herself what all this was leading up to. Brett had made his interests clear enough. What he needed was to be brought up short, and she would take pleasure in doing it. Only not just yet. Let him simmer a while in anticipation. The rebuttal would come all the harder.

Whatever his intentions, he was an excellent host. Several times during the meal, Lisa found herself forgetting why she was here and simply enjoyed his company. In normal circumstances, she could easily become enamoured, she acknowledged wryly at one point, watching his face as he talked. He radiated such masculine charisma.

It wasn't all agreement by any means. They held differing opinions on many things. Brett appeared to relish the arguments.

'You're stubborn as a mule,' he declared without rancour at one point.

Other issues forgotten for the moment, Lisa gave a laugh. 'The pot calling the kettle black!'

His grin was easy. 'So we're two of a kind.' He reached for the wine decanter. 'Your glass is nearly empty.'

For the third time, she realised, yet she felt no ill-effects from what she had drunk. On the contrary, she felt on top of the world, her mind clear as crystal.

'I won't have any more, thanks,' she said decisively, not wanting to risk spoiling this mood.

Brett made no effort to persuade her, nor did he bother refilling his own glass.

'It's turned cooler,' he observed. 'Why don't we have coffee inside?'

If the warning bells sounded at all they were too far off at the moment to have any impact. Lisa nodded her agreement, happy to wait for him to come round and pull out her chair. He had proved himself so different from prior impressions this past hour or two. A man of many facets was Brett Sanderson, and disarming with it.

The sliding glass doors gave access to a spacious living-room furnished and decorated in the light and airy style that went so well with the climate. Lisa trod across the thickly piled expanse of off-white carpet to sink into one of several scattered sofas, eyeing the wide stone hearth at present holding an arrangement of tropical greenery.

'I shouldn't have imagined you'd ever need fires here,' she commented.

'We don't,' Brett confirmed. 'But I like a focal point in a room. A left-over from my English childhood maybe.'

The man who had served them dinner brought coffee through on a wagon, revealing no surprise at finding them indoors.

'You can get off now, Sol,' said Brett casually.

'Sol?' Lisa queried after he had gone.

'Short for Solomon. Biblical names are popular in the islands. Are you going to pour, or shall I?'

'You do it,' she invited. 'I'd hate to spill any on the carpet.'

'I dare say it would clean.' From his tone, such matters were of little concern. 'Black or white?'

'White, please,' she requested. 'And one sugar.'

'A woman after my own heart,' he remarked on a light note, handing her the delicate china cup and saucer.

But unlikely to reach it, came the thought, and she felt her spirits suddenly plummet.

Refusing the brandy on offer, she took a second cup of coffee instead. Not that she needed to sober up at all; she had never felt more so. If Brett intended the evening to end the way she had suspected all along, then the move had to come soon. How she was going to handle it she wasn't yet sure. The only thing she was sure of was her ultimate answer.

Suspicion crystallised into certainty when he took the empty cup from her and dropped into a seat at her side.

'I've waited long enough,' he said softly.

Lisa steeled herself against the almost overpowering temptation to allow him at least a little leeway. Once started, he might well refuse to take no for an answer. If the truth were known, she wasn't all that sure of her own strength of mind where he was concerned. He made her feel like throwing caution to the winds.

'Is this where I start paying for my supper?' she asked as he slid a hand beneath the heavy fall of her hair to tilt her face towards his.

His smile faded. For a long moment he just sat there looking at her, eyes narrowed, face set in lines she hadn't seen all evening. When he spoke his voice lacked any hint of softness.

'Is that what you expect to do?'

'It's what I think you expect,' she said, struggling to maintain some command over the situation. 'Isn't that why you told Sol to go?'

The hand at her neck was abruptly removed. 'I told Sol to go because his job was finished. As to the other, I won't deny wanting to make love to you, but it takes two in the same frame of mind in my book. I'm not into rape—or seduction either, if it comes to that.'

'I'm sorry.' The apology came hard.

'So am I,' he clipped. 'I think it's time you went.'

'Not like this.' She was suddenly desperate to put things right between them again. 'Brett, I made a mistake. Accept my apology—please!'

About to get up, he subsided again, though his face remained set, his eyes cool. 'Give me one good reason why I should.'

'Because I'm asking you to,' was all she could come up with.

'Why?'

She gazed at him, searching her mind for something—anything—that might suffice to undo the damage. She had been so wrong about him, so utterly and completely influenced by preconceptions. He could hardly be blamed for feeling the way he did.

'What do you want me to say?' she appealed. 'You already know I'm attracted to you.'

'But you don't trust me,' he said flatly.

'I do now.' Lisa put out a hand and touched the firm lips, tremoring at the very feel of them. 'I really do, Brett.'

For a moment he remained motionless, face unrelenting, then his mouth softened, lips opening to take her fingertip between them in a gesture that set her pulses racing. The grey eyes were fathomless; she felt herself drowning in them.

She put up no resistance when he gathered her to him, sliding her arms about his neck to give herself over to the long, searching kiss, feeling the warmth spreading through her, the curling sensation deep in the pit of her stomach, the heady emotion taking over her mind. She found herself clinging to him, opening her lips to the questing, spine-tingling intrusion of his tongue; felt the blood racing like fire through her veins.

The touch of his hand at her breast was no shock but a natural and much desired progression. She shifted position instinctively to allow him full access, thrilling to the knowledgeable caress. She wanted this man; she had wanted him the whole time. She was ready to admit it now. Who cared about afterwards?

When he unfastened her top two shirt buttons and slid his hand inside to find bare flesh she was in total if tremoring accord. Her nipple peaked beneath his sensitive fingers, the pleasure so intense she could hardly bear it. She slipped her own fingers between the buttons of his shirt to feel the wiry curl of hair on his chest, the warmth of his skin, the beat of his heart, yearning for some closer contact. Her whole body ached with the need of it.

It was Brett who called a halt, pulling her clothing back into place and putting her firmly away from him.

'I think you'd better go.'

She gazed at him with darkened eyes, grappling with the realisation that he meant it.

'Don't look so distressed,' he said drily. 'You're leaving as you came. That was what you wanted, wasn't it?'

Lisa got abruptly to her feet, conscious of a weakness in her lower limbs. She felt disgusted with herself. All that fine talk, and what had she proved?

'I hope you rot in hell!' she jerked out through stiff lips.

He came upright himself, his smile sardonic. 'I dare say your wish will be fulfilled. I'll watch you down the steps.'

'I can see myself out, thanks,' she gritted.

'I always see my guests off the premises,' he returned unequivocally. 'Without exception.'

They walked in silence across the patio. Brett had his hands in his trouser pockets and an enigmatic expression on his face. He came to a halt at the head of the flight of steps, eyes unrevealing in the deck lighting.

'Sweet dreams,' he said. 'And watch your step.'

Lisa descended blindly, hardly caring whether she got down safely or not. That last had sounded like a threat. Either she toed the line from now on, or else. Whichever way she took it, it was obvious that there would be no further personal involvement. His masculine pride had been salved. End of story.

That the word had spread was evident from the glances cast her way the following day, the whispered comments. Selina was the only one to speak openly on the subject.

'Who do you plan on dating next?' she asked over lunch.

'I don't make plans,' Lisa replied with what equability she could muster. 'I'm not sure what you've heard, but it will almost certainly have been exaggerated.'

'Sol says you and the boss man were real pally last night when he left. How does he rate?'

Lisa kept her tone even. 'As a perfect host, and a thorough gentleman, as you'd expect.'

Selina grinned, showing a perfect set of gleaming white teeth. 'I meant in the sack.'

'You've picked up far too many coarse Americanisms. Brett—Mr Sanderson asked me to have dinner with him because we're both English. A friendly gesture, that's all.'

'Real friendly.' It was obvious that the other woman didn't believe it for a moment. 'I'll spread the word around.'

'I'd as soon you didn't bother. It isn't that important.'

The grin came again. 'Whatever you say.'

Lisa left it there. Whatever the rumours going around, she could do little to put a stop to them. They would die a natural death once it was realised that her suspected affair with the Royale's owner was not ongoing. In the meantime, she would simply have to ignore it all.

What she hadn't counted on was Richard's getting to hear of it. He had made an appointment for Wednesday morning, having been bothered with some stiffness in his shoulder again. As usual he requested treatment in his suite.

'What's this I hear about you and Brett?' he asked as she worked on him. 'Do I detect a budding romance?'

'It isn't like that,' said Lisa shortly. 'I'd have thought you above listening to idle gossip!'

He levered himself up on an elbow to look at her, eyebrows raised. 'Something wrong?'

She made a wry gesture, aware of having given herself away. 'Nothing I can't handle.'

'Do you want to talk about it?' he invited. 'It some-times helps.'

Lisa smiled faintly. 'It's not worth talking about, but thanks anyway.'

'He's hurt you, hasn't he?' The question was sharp.

'No!' Her voice was equally sharp. 'I already told you, it isn't like that!'

'Then why so cut up?' he insisted. He pressed himself upright, swinging his legs over the edge of the treatment table to sit looking at her with perspicacity. 'You're in love with him, aren't you?'

Lisa's heart did a painful double beat. 'I most cer-tainly am not!' she snapped. 'I hardly know the man!'

'So how long does it take?' came the unmoved re-sponse. 'I fell in love with my wife the first time I set eyes on her. And I was still in love with her when she died, in case you've any doubts about the lasting quality. Brett's a fine man.'

'I wouldn't dispute it.' She was doing her best to take control of her emotions. 'But I'm no more in love with him than he is with me. All we did was have dinner together.'

'And he never even so much as kissed you?' Richard gave a sage little smile as her colour came up. 'I take it you had no objections at the time?'

'Finding a man attractive is a long way from being in love with him,' Lisa responded, abandoning any further attempt at denial. 'In any case, it won't be happening again.'

'You mean he tried to go too far too soon?'

'On the contrary, he——' She broke off, biting her lip. 'Look, I appreciate your interest, Richard, but I really don't want to talk about it. All right?'

'Of course.' He wasn't in the least put out. 'Just remember, I'm here if you change your mind.' He swung himself back on to the table again. 'In the meantime, there's still my shoulder.'

Lisa went back to work feeling anything but composed. It was ridiculous to suggest that she might be in love with Brett. More so than Richard could possibly know. No man who could do what he had done to her last night was worth a second thought. All she needed was to get a grip on herself.

Which was easier said than done, but she managed it to a great degree over the course of the week. Whether Brett had returned to Boston or was still on site she didn't know and made no attempt to find out. By the time she saw him again she wanted to be in total control of her emotions. Hating him was a complete waste of time and effort. Indifference was what she had to aim for.

She had dinner with Richard one evening, and agreed to accompany him on the snorkelling trip the coming Saturday. He was a very different character from her own father, but she was beginning to feel very fond of him. His relationship with his son wasn't in the same category as that which he had shared with Helen, he told her. There was little depth of understanding between them.

Probably his own fault for being so tied up in business matters during Lance's formative years, he acknowledged. He had found more time for Helen. Listening to him, Lisa could only be grateful for the time and attention her father had given all his family. She had never realised before that it could be any other way.

Relations with Gary Conway were far from easy, although he made no further attempt to force the issue over her continuing association with Richard. Popular as she was proving to be with the clientele, he could hardly justify terminating her employment either. That decision would rest with Brett when the time came.

True to pattern, the gossip died a natural death from lack of further stimulation. She was even accorded a certain sympathy by one or two of the female staff, as the supposed victim of typical male exploitation. Lisa didn't even attempt to correct the notion. Denials only served to fuel the fire.

The weekend came round again fast. With no less than a dozen people taking advantage of the *Seajade*'s availability, transport was laid on from the hotel to the marina where the yacht was berthed. Joining Richard outside the main doors at eight-thirty, Lisa was conscious of some speculative glances from others in the group, but turned a blind eye. She was becoming inured to it all.

The *Seajade* proved to be a sixty-foot ketch, her white hull and warm teak decks gleaming invitingly in the morning sunlight. They weren't to have the boat to themselves, Lisa realised on seeing other people already on board. Not that space was so limited, she supposed.

Those of them without rope-soled deck shoes were requested to go barefoot in order not to damage the lovingly preserved teak. Lisa could find no quarrel with that ruling, though a couple of the older women made no secret of their disapproval. The discarded footwear was left in a basket placed ready on the jetty. Insurance against temptation, Lisa surmised. Some people were capable of disregarding directives on principal, given half a chance.

It was only when actually on board, with her own shoes ready stored, that she spotted the familiar figure up front. Brett was talking with a young couple dressed as he was himself in shorts and T-shirt, an arm slung casually about Andrea Gordon's tanned shoulders. His back was turned, the dark head slightly bent as if to catch what was being said. Lisa felt her insides turn fluid as his laugh rang out.

'You didn't tell me *he* was going to be here too,' she accused Richard. 'I'm getting off!'

'It's too late,' he said. 'We're already casting off.' He made an apologetic gesture. 'I didn't even know he was down again, much less that he'd be joining us. Not that he doesn't have the right. It *is* his boat.'

His boat, his world, thought Lisa painfully, and she belonged in neither.

CHAPTER SIX

WITH a crew of three, there was no call on the boat's owner to do anything but play host to his guests. They were clear of the marina before Brett began to mingle with the rest of the party, most of whom he appeared to be on easy terms with.

Lisa steeled herself to meet his gaze steadily when he reached her, surprised by his lack of surprise on seeing her sitting there on the cushioned sundeck.

'Have you done much snorkelling?' he asked.

'None at all,' she admitted. 'But I'm game to try it.'

His smile was dry. 'There's little danger if you follow the rules. Richard will tell you what they are.'

'I've only been out the one time myself,' the latter disclaimed. 'It would be better coming from you.'

'Or anyone else with experience,' put in Lisa swiftly. 'I'm sure Mr Sanderson can find better things to do than teach beginners the ropes.'

The spark that leapt in the grey eyes was not imagined. 'On the contrary, I consider it my responsibility to make sure everyone on board knows exactly what they're doing. We'll be making our first stop soon. I'll see you then.'

Richard waited until he was out of earshot before saying softly, 'If you're trying to rile him, I'd guess you're going the right way about it. You don't call a man who's kissed you "Mr" without asking for retaliation.'

'He's my employer,' she returned. 'What else should I call him?'

'Stop playing dumb,' he admonished. 'You know what I'm talking about. Whatever happened between the two of you, it obviously cut deep.'

Lisa gave in, her smile wry. 'For me, perhaps, not for him.'

'Don't be too sure. The way he looked at you just now, he's no way unresponsive.'

To deliberated provocation perhaps, Lisa reflected, but no more than that. Indifference was difficult to achieve when his very presence made her tense up this way. The day stretching ahead had lost much of its appeal.

Nevertheless, the sheer enjoyment to be found skimming over the sparkling waters couldn't be denied. Dark glasses were a necessity, Lisa realised, dazzled by the reflection when she removed hers for a moment or two. There seemed to be islands everywhere she looked, some no more than a rocky protuberance, others green and verdant against the backcloth of vivid blue sky.

'I can understand why sailing is so popular a sport,' she commented to Richard. 'Especially in a climate like this.' She looked up at the tall white sails billowing in the wind, enjoying the smooth swooping movement as they breasted the waves. 'I never did any before.'

'Glad you came after all, then?' he asked slyly, and she gave a rueful little laugh.

'At the moment I am.'

Her eyes sought out the familiar figure among the group forward of where they were seated. Brett looked so relaxed, so much at home in this environment. Sticking close to his side, Andrea had already removed her top and shorts to reveal a minuscule bikini almost the same colour as her skin. As near nude as it was possible to get without going the whole way, Lisa reflected, yet she seemed totally without self-consciousness.

They dropped anchor for the first time over a reef some few hundred yards out from a rocky islet. Masks with snorkel tubes ready attached were provided for everyone on board, along with the ungainly swimming-fins.

'It might be a good idea to keep your T-shirt on,' said Richard as Lisa slipped off her shorts. 'It's very easy to get your back burnt.'

One or two of the others were keeping theirs on too, she noted, accepting the advice. She had never used fins before either, and found them difficult to put on, even more so to stand up in.

'I feel like a penguin!' she laughed. 'How on earth do I make it into the water?'

'A step at a time,' said Brett, coming up in time to catch the last. 'Have you tried your mask on yet?'

Lisa shook her head, not caring to speak. She didn't look at him when he took the mask from her and slipped the strap over her head, fighting the claustrophobic sensation as the rubber flange clamped to her face.

He had stripped down to black trunks himself. His naked chest was only inches from her eyes as he adjusted the strap. The wiry curl of hair bore a faint sheen of perspiration, creating a sudden wild and unprecedented urge in her to lean forward and taste the salty flavour on her lips.

The tube thrust into her mouth both felt and tasted totally alien. It was only with a real effort that she resisted the urge to spit it straight out again, taking in air as instructed. She was going to master this technique if it killed her!

'We have a couple of inflatable vests on board if you feel in need of some extra support,' he said. 'How good a swimmer are you?'

Lisa took the tube from her mouth in order to answer, not about to suffer the indignity of a life-jacket. 'Good enough.'

Richard started to say something, then obviously thought better of it. Brett gave her a narrowed look.

'You'll be buddying with me for now,' he declared in a manner brooking no argument. 'Richard, you go with Dave over there. If you both shape up OK, you can team up together this afternoon.'

'Will do,' agreed Richard amiably. 'See you later,' he added to Lisa.

'Take your mask off and spit on the inside glass,' Brett instructed. 'Rub it round with your finger and it will stop the glass misting up when you're under water.'

Lisa did so, too intent on keeping her reactions to him under strict control to be nervous of this plunge into the unknown. Most of the others were already in the water. She tensed involuntarily when he took hold of her arm.

'I'm giving you a hand down on to the platform,' he said with irony, 'not making a pass. Relax, will you?'

'I can manage,' she asserted.

'Fine.' He let go of her, standing back to give her room. 'So let's see you do it.'

She managed to make it out on to the narrow diving platform without mishap; she even managed to descend the first two rungs of the short ladder, pausing to don the mask and take the snorkel tube into her mouth. Drawing in a steadying breath, she lowered herself all the way into the wonderfully warm water and pushed off, hands by her sides, face down, legs stretched out straight behind her as she had seen the others do.

It was a whole different world down there—a fantasy world of colour and movement. There were blue fish and striped fish, fish that changed colour as they altered direction, some so large they might be scary if they weren't so lovely, others so tiny they looked like bits of quicksilver. The sensation, gazing down through the thirty feet or more of crystal-clear water, was like flying under one's own power over a landscape drawn by artists.

Brett came up alongside her, touching her chin in a signal to lift her head.

'OK?' he asked, removing the tube from his mouth.

Lisa did the same, too overwhelmed with the wonder of it all to be constrained with him. 'It's fantastic!' she exclaimed.

There was no telling what his expression might be behind the concealing mask, but his nod was tolerant. 'If you want to try diving, don't forget to blow out your tube when you surface. I'll be right here if you get into any difficulties.'

It was reassuring to know that. Lisa replaced the tube, then took a deep breath and up-ended, amazed by the difference the fins made to her movement through the water. She didn't get right down to the white sand so far below, but managed a creditable distance, delighted to find that, far from scattering, the fish kept on swimming all around her. One tiger-striped specimen actually nuzzled her outstretched fingers before moving on to look for more edible food elsewhere.

'You're doing brilliantly,' Brett encouraged her when she surfaced again. 'Ten more minutes, then we go back on board. It's easy to over-extend yourself when you're not used to it.'

'I don't want to spoil things for you,' she said, treading water. 'I can cope on my own now.'

'You never, in any circumstances, do this without a partner,' he stated. 'It's the oldest rule in the book. There'll be another session after lunch. I can wait till then.'

Buddying with Andrea, no doubt, thought Lisa with a sudden return to reality. From what she had seen, the other woman was an expert.

It seemed more like ten seconds than minutes when Brett indicated that it was time to return to the boat. He hoisted himself up to the diving deck first, tossing his fins and mask on to the main deck and turning back to look down on her clinging to the ladder below.

'Take off your fins first,' he instructed, 'and sling them up to me.'

She did so with difficulty, almost dropping one of them in the process. Brett disposed of them the same way he had done with his own, then extended a hand to draw her bodily up the ladder on to the deck.

For a timeless moment she was held close to the broad, water-beaded chest as he balanced to the movement of the boat—felt the sudden tingling in her nipples as they brushed against him. She was wearing a bikini-top beneath the clinging T-shirt, but it made little difference.

'Nice,' he said softly.

Face hot beneath the mask still in place, Lisa pushed past him. Apart from the crew, everyone was still in the water. She seized a towel, ripping off the mask and attacking her dripping hair with a vigour verging on savagery. Why couldn't he just leave her alone?

'I'm hardly going to be following up the invitation here,' he said with irony, 'so you can come out from under that towel.'

She did so, eyes blazing as she looked up into the lean brown features, hair tumbled about her face. '*What* invitation?'

His mouth slanted. 'You know what I'm talking about. You just don't want to admit to it.'

The sight of Andrea hoisting herself up to the diving platform froze any reply Lisa might have made in her throat. Mask in hand, the newcomer looked anything but pleased to see the two of them standing so close.

'Are you coming back in, Brett?' she called.

His smile easy, he nodded agreement and took up his equipment again. 'Have a rest now and you'll be ready to try it again this afternoon,' he said. 'Lunch in half an hour.'

Eating was the last thing on Lisa's mind as she watched him follow Andrea down the ladder. The brunette obviously only had to beckon. Not that it made any difference to her own situation. Brett might feel moved to taunt her, but that was as far as it went.

And that, she vowed fiercely, was as far as she wanted it to go!

Others started filtering back on board. One of the older women, whom Lisa had treated on several occasions, came over to sit with her.

'Isn't this just great?' she enthused. 'Brett sure knows how to take care of his guests! I've spent these same weeks at the Royale the last three years since the place opened, but this is the first time we've met. Somebody said he usually comes down over the Christmas period. Do you happen to know if he's planning on doing that this year?'

'I'm afraid I've no idea.' Lisa kept her tone neutral. 'Why don't you ask him?'

'I will. I was planning to spend Christmas with some friends in Barbados, but they've had to change their plans, so I may stay on here myself.'

This was the same woman that Richard had said was on the look-out for a new husband, Lisa recalled. If she had her sights set on Brett she would be in for another disappointment, well-preserved though she was for her forty-five or more years.

Prepared in a galley scarcely large enough to swing a cat in, the buffet luncheon set out in the spacious cockpit was superb. Along with the food was a full choice of drinks, from champagne right through to fruit juice and mineral water. Lisa stuck to the latter for the simple reason that she wanted to keep a clear head for the afternoon session, but few of the others seemed concerned.

'We'll be moving on to another location, so it's going to be an hour or two before we go in again,' Richard advised when she mentioned the matter. He was drinking the light American beer himself. 'I wouldn't mind trying scuba-diving after this,' he added. 'How about you?'

Lisa laughed, shaking her head. 'I'm happy enough with this for the time being.'

Seated near by, Brett gave her a mocking glance. 'Where's your spirit of adventure?'

'Kept within reasonable bounds,' she retorted levelly.

'How sensible to know your own limitations,' drawled Andrea with deceptive laziness. And how dull, was the intimation. She was probably right at that.

'Will you be coming down over Christmas this year, Brett?' asked the woman Lisa had been speaking with earlier on a casual note.

'I may do,' he returned equally casually. 'Depends how things work out.'

With business, or with Andrea? Lisa wondered, and felt the deep-down pang.

They upped anchor at one o'clock, and spent an hour or so sailing before hoving to again in a little cove. The crescent of silver-white beach tempted one or two people to forsake snorkelling in favour of shell-gathering or simply lazing around under the palms, but Lisa was more than ready to join Richard in a renewal of the morning's delights.

The thickets of kelp covering the bottom here created a totally different though equally fascinating environment. Lisa was enchanted by her first glimpse of the tiny sea-horses nodding along like so many escapees from Disney World.

Gaining confidence, she found swimming under water so much easier than the morning. As the whole group was staying fairly close together, the 'buddying' principle didn't seem quite so important. She forgot about it altogether in following a school of brilliant blue parrot fish in their lazy meanderings, only realising that she had been moving inshore when the kelp eventually gave way to bare sand and the water shallowed.

Intending to take a breather before swimming back to the boat, she found her feet and waded out, pulling off her mask as she did so. At first glance it seemed that everyone else had already returned to the boat, as the beach was deserted. Except that it wasn't the same beach, she realised with a sense of shock, taking in the subtle differences. She must have swum round into the adjoining cove.

Right at this moment she felt physically incapable of making it back on her own. Her legs were shaky, the muscles aching a little. It had been utterly stupid of her not to take occasional bearings, she knew, but the sea surface was so calm, there had been no need to lift her face out of the water at all during the last ten or fifteen minutes in order to breathe.

A few minutes' rest and she would be fine, she reassured herself. Having got here in the first place, she could obviously get back without difficulty. Just a few hundred yards, that was all. No great distance with the aid of the fins.

She lay out flat on the soft sand to relax her muscles, eyes closed against the sun. The first she knew of another presence was when a shadow fell across her. Dripping water, Brett towered over her, his expression grim.

'What the hell do you think you're playing at?' he demanded.

Lisa came upright with a jerk. 'I got a bit off-track,' she said huskily. 'Foolish, I know, but——'

'Idiotic would be closer to the mark,' came the terse interruption. 'If I hadn't spotted you heading round here we'd have thought you'd been caught up somewhere!'

'I'm sorry,' she said, not about to dispute the point. 'I was following a shoal of fish and just didn't realise how far I'd come. I'm ready to go back now.'

'You'll stay put until *I* say you're ready,' he commanded. 'I've no intention of towing you back.'

Blue eyes flashed as anger overrode apology. 'I've no intention of letting you! In fact, I'd as soon not have you near me at all!'

'Is that so?' His voice had gone dangerously quiet, the slant of his lips a warning in itself. 'Then prove it to me.'

Lisa went rigid as he dropped down over her, pushing her back on to the sand. The leg he slung across hers made escape impossible, even if he had given her the time to think about it. His mouth was scorching, cutting through her defences to reach the very core of her being—arousing a response that took little note of her desperate attempt to control it.

The anger in him gave way to something infinitely more disturbing as he sensed her resistance ebbing away. She found her lips opening to him of their own accord, her whole body shuddering to the touch of his tongue on the soft inner flesh. No harsh intrusion but a delicate seeking that made her want to answer in kind, to taste him the way he was tasting her.

The evocative male scent of him filled her nostrils, drawing an even deeper response. She moved instinctively against him, seeking closer contact with the hard angles of his body, trembling to the feel of him when he accommodated that desire. The hand slipped beneath the elasticated band of her bikini-top to find her bare breast was so sensitive in its caress. Then the hand was gone and his mouth was there instead, forcing a bubbling little cry from her lips as she clutched wildly at the wet, dark head.

'Tell me now that you don't want me!' he said roughly against her skin. 'Tell me, Lisa!'

He was doing this only to prove a point, that part of her mind still rational enough to think at all reminded her. If she told him what he wanted to hear, he would have every excuse to taking things to their natural conclusion. It was what she wanted too, only it wasn't going to happen. She wouldn't allow it to happen!

'I may not be totally immune to your degree of expertise,' she forced out, 'but I can still say no and mean it!'

'The way you did the other night?' His tone was harsh. 'I could have taken you then, and you know it!'

'Then perhaps you should have done,' she flung at him recklessly. 'Because you're not getting another chance! I'd see you in hell before I'd give you the satisfaction!'

He lifted himself up a little to look at her, his mouth savage. 'Don't pressure me. I'm just about at the end of my rope with you!'

'Is that a fact?' She was too incensed to pay any heed to the very real threat. 'And how am I supposed to feel?'

His eyes bored into hers. 'Why don't you tell me?'

'I hate your guts!' Her voice shook with the force of it. 'You're the most despicable, contemptible man I ever met, and I wish to God I never had!'

'But you still want me.' The anger had given way to an infinitely more disturbing emotion. 'The same way I want you—the way I've wanted you for the past two weeks, damn it!'

Lisa lay motionless under him, feeling the potent weight of him bearing her down. The sand was packed firm beneath her, its trapped heat a spur to that gathering inside her. Her hands lifted of their own accord to slide over the broad, bare shoulders, feeling the muscle ripple under her fingers. She was drowning in the depths of his eyes again, and suddenly no longer caring.

'Not here,' he said softly. 'They'll be sending out search parties any minute.' He dropped his head and found her mouth in a kiss that was both seal and promise, before pushing himself upright. 'Tomorrow we're going to spend the day together. Just the two of us.'

Lisa sat up as he got to his feet, pulling her bikini-top back into place with unsteady hands. She had given too much away to start trying to retract, but that didn't mean she was ready to fall in with his plans.

'I don't think so,' she said.

'What are you afraid of?' he demanded.

Of being hurt, she could have told him. 'If I keep my job I want it to be on the strength of my professional performance,' she returned with deliberation. 'You can find far better exponents of the other kind, I'm sure.'

He reached down and drew her to her feet, his expression determined. 'If a performance were all I was looking for, I could have stayed in Boston. And your job in no way depends on your coming through for me.'

She looked back at him unflinchingly. 'In that case, why keep me on tenterhooks? I've already proved myself.'

His jaw set. 'Don't make the job an issue, Lisa. I said six weeks.'

In other words, no promises. That wasn't his way. If she gave way to temptation and responded to him the way she so desperately wanted to respond, everything else had to take a back seat. Whatever his motives, it was unlikely that he contemplated an ongoing relationship.

If he had kissed her again that might have been the deciding factor, but he didn't.

'We'd better be getting back,' he said flatly instead. 'Let's get you geared up again.'

He paced himself to stay with her as they swam back around the little headland. Only when they were within easy reach of the boat did he forge ahead to hoist himself out of the water and offer her a helping hand.

Richard was already back on board, and blaming himself for letting her out of his sight.

'One minute you were there, the next gone!' he said. 'I'd never have forgiven myself if anything had happened to you!'

'It was my own fault,' Lisa assured him. 'I forgot the rules. Anyway, I'm fine.'

'A good thing Brett saw you going, or you might not have been.'

'No harm done,' said Brett. Grey eyes met blue for a brief moment, then he moved away, leaving her torn with doubt as to what message he had been conveying. There was every chance that he already regretted what he had said back there.

Changed now out of the flesh-coloured bikini into shorts and T-shirt again, Andrea gave her a thoughtful scrutiny. Lisa returned her gaze expressionlessly, looking away without haste. There lay another good reason for not getting personally involved with Brett. He might want her physically, but Andrea was more his kind.

They were hit by a sudden squall on the way back to St Thomas. Seeing it coming at them across the water, Lisa realised for the first time how totally unpredictable the sea's moods could be.

Unlike some of the others who retired below to ride out the storm, she chose to stay where she was. The coldness of the rain when it hit them took her breath for a moment or two, but it didn't last long, and the *Seajade* easily weathered the wind-driven waves. She even found the increased motion exhilarating.

'A glutton for punishment,' commented Richard, coming back on deck after the squall had passed to find her soaked to the skin. 'It's to be hoped you don't pick up a chill.'

With the decks already steaming in the sun, Lisa doubted it. Brett had stayed up top too, but he hadn't come near her, substantiating her belief that he had decided against pursuing matters any further. No great loss, she told herself stoutly. It would have been a short-lived

affair at best—with every possibility of receiving her
marching orders because of it, regardless of what he had
said.

They made the harbour just before five, dispersing to
their various modes of transport. Lisa tried to stay in-
different when she saw Brett putting Andrea into the
passenger seat of a red Ferrari, but it was a losing battle.
They would be spending the evening together, and
probably the night too, as no doubt they often did. If
she had agreed to see him tomorrow she would have had
that thought in mind all day.

Too tired after the long day to consider going far,
Richard opted for dinner in the restaurant. Lisa declined
to join him on the grounds that she wasn't hungry, and
spent the whole evening writing letters to friends and
family, assailed by homesickness. This opportunity had
seemed heaven-sent at the time, but right now she wished
she had never come.

As on the previous occasion, she was in bed when the
telephone rang. For a moment or two she considered
ignoring it, but that proved impossible.

'Sorry to leave it so late,' said Brett, 'but I only just
got in. Come up to the house about eight and have
breakfast while we decide how we're going to spend the
day. Bring a suit, and we can take a swim before we eat.'

Pulses leaping all over the place, Lisa said thickly,
'You're taking a lot for granted.'

'I want to see you.' His voice was lower, his tone com-
pelling. 'You didn't really think I was going to give up
that easily?'

'What about Andrea?' The words were torn from her.

'I'm not answerable to Andrea.' The statement was
all the more meaningful for its lack of force. There was

a pause before he added softly, 'What happened to that reckless streak?'

She was fighting it right this moment, she could have told him—and losing too. The chances of developing a lasting relationship might be just about non-existent, but if she turned away from him now she would spend the rest of her life wondering what she'd missed.

'I'm going to take it that the answer is yes,' he said when she failed to reply. 'Don't let me down.'

Lying there in the darkness after he had rung off, Lisa wondered what he might do if she didn't turn up. Not that she had any real intention of putting him to the test. Tomorrow at some point they would make love; he had made it very clear that that was where his interests lay. She wanted it too. More than she had ever wanted anything. There was every possibility that she would finish up getting hurt, but she would deal with that if and when it happened. Caution was for the cautious.

CHAPTER SEVEN

AWAKE half the night, Lisa was dismayed to find it was already gone eight when she surfaced from sleep. She showered quickly, and donned a bikini under her light cotton tunic in anticipation of the swim to come, packing bra and briefs in a tote bag for later. Whatever the outcome, she was going to make the most of today, she thought, viewing her sun-bronzed face and sparkling eyes in the mirror.

She was on her way to the door when the telephone rang.

'I overslept,' she announced, taking it for granted who would be calling at this hour. 'I'll be there in a few minutes.'

'You'd better be,' came the tolerant reply. 'Patience isn't one of my virtues.'

Lisa laughed, warmed by the very sound of Brett's voice. 'You'll have to practise more.'

'Meaning you're in the habit of keeping a man waiting?'

'A woman's prerogative,' she rejoined lightly.

'Not one I recognise, so take heed.' His tone was mock-serious. 'You've got ten minutes.'

She might have made it if she hadn't bumped into Gary Conway while taking a short cut through the lobby.

'You'd no business going out on *Seajade* yesterday,' he said without preamble. 'She's strictly for the use of paying guests.'

'I was invited by a paying guest,' Lisa responded.

'That's not the point. How do you think the rest of the staff feel about it?'

'I haven't asked them.' She hesitated, recognising the validity in what he was saying yet at something of a loss as to what to do about it. 'Brett didn't seem to object,' was all she could come up with.

'You think you've got both him and Hanson wrapped round your little finger, don't you?' he snapped. 'I dare say you might have in Hanson's case, but you can forget any hopes you might be entertaining in Brett's direction. He's hardly likely to settle for little Miss Nobody!'

Lisa made every effort to retain an outer poise. 'I'm sure you're right. But then I don't happen to consider myself a nobody.'

Gary's colour deepened a little beneath his tan. When he spoke again it was in a more muted note. 'I'm directly responsible for your being here, Lisa. I don't want to see you get hurt.'

The sudden change of mood was disconcerting. Lisa hardly knew how to react. 'If I'm what you think I am, why should it worry you?' she said stiffly.

'I'd have thought that pretty obvious.' His tone was wry. 'You gave me every reason to believe we had something going for us back in London. Why else would I have gone out on a limb to get you here? You're good at what you do, sure, but I could have found someone closer to home.'

Lisa gazed at him unhappily. 'If I did give that impression then it was totally unintentional. I liked you, of course. We seemed to get along so well. I just never imagined——'

'It's so much water under the bridge now,' he interrupted with a return to brusqueness. 'Brett's going back to Boston again in the morning, in case you didn't know.'

He moved off, leaving her standing there biting her lip. It was only to be expected that Brett would be going back again, of course. She simply hadn't thought beyond today. Christmas was only a couple of weeks away. If he planned on spending it here, as he had intimated he might yesterday, it was unlikely that he would be down again next weekend.

So what? she asked herself resolutely. She already knew the odds against any emotional development on Brett's part. He wanted her the way he might want any woman he found physically attractive, and once he'd had her could well lose interest—but she was prepared to take that risk. No other man had ever made her feel the way he did; she had begun to consider herself incapable of such feelings. To know what true fulfilment was like even once was better than never knowing it at all.

A good fifteen minutes had passed before she finally reached the patio. Stretched out on one of the padded lounges, hands behind his head, Brett regarded her with quizzically lifted brows.

'Making a point?'

'Gary wanted a word,' she said. 'I don't go in for those kind of games.'

'I'm glad to hear it.' He came to his feet, lithe as a panther in the plain black trunks he seemed to favour. 'Coming in?'

It took her only a moment to peel off the white tunic. Her blue and white figured bikini was nowhere near as brief as the one Andrea had worn yesterday, but still more revealing than anything she had owned before. The look in Brett's eyes as he studied her slender shape was a boost to her confidence, enabling her to give him a deliberately tantalising little smile as she strolled to the pool-edge.

Having tried diving on only a few occasions back home, Lisa knew it was perhaps foolish to take a header into the water now instead of using the steps, but she managed an astonishingly smooth entry. Brett was nowhere to be seen when she surfaced. Only on feeling the hands fastening about her waist from behind did she realise that he must have dived in immediately after her.

He drew her back against him, treading water for them both as he put his lips to the nape of her neck where the hair had parted. 'Those who tease pay the penalty,' he said softly. 'You've been warned.'

Lisa hardly cared. The feel of his hands on her tremored every nerve in her body. If he had made any further move she wasn't sure what she would have done, but he released her, swimming away in a fast crawl that took him to the other end of the pool in seconds. Arms slung over the brass rail in support, he looked back at her.

'Try a couple of lengths. You need to build up your muscle strength.'

He was right about that. Without fins on her feet, Lisa found her progress very much slower and far more strenuous than yesterday's. The crawl was beyond her; she had to settle for the unspectacular breast-stroke instead.

'We're like the tortoise and the hare,' she said with an attempt at humour when she finally completed the second length. 'I feel a real drag!'

'The tortoise won in the end,' Brett pointed out. 'All you need is practice. Feel free to use the pool any time.'

'Gary won't approve,' she responded lightly, and saw his jaw firm.

'I'll deal with Gary.'

He hoisted himself out of the water, standing up to offer her a hand. Lisa took it, thrilling once more to the power in him as he drew her up on to the pool-edge. For a brief, quivering moment they were close, but he made no attempt to prolong the contact.

'There's a spare robe on the chair over there,' he said. 'Do you want to eat outdoors or in?'

'Out,' she chose, not really caring where they ate—or even if.

Brett gave her an approving smile. 'Decisiveness— that's what I like in a woman!'

'We aim to please,' she returned, employing the same light tone.

Grey eyes took on a spine-tingling warmth. 'You do.'

If he'd kissed her then she would have melted in his arms, but once again he forbore. Moving to the indicated chair, he took up one of the two towelling robes and held it out for her to slide her arms into the sleeves, then donned the other garment himself. Hers was much smaller than his, Lisa realised. A woman's size. But then why not? She was hardly the first woman he had entertained up here, in the pool or out of it.

Forget about the others, she instructed herself firmly. Right now Brett wanted *her* company. That was all she cared about.

He prepared breakfast himself in the spacious, beautifully equipped kitchen, grilling bacon and scrambling eggs with an efficiency Lisa doubted she could have bettered, even if allowed. She was accustomed to nothing more than coffee and toast in the morning as a general rule, but the sizzling aromas made her mouth water.

'Exercise creates healthy appetites,' agreed Brett when she said as much. He tipped the pan of hash browns into the partitioned, heated dish, and put on the lid. 'Right, you carry the plates and juice jug, and I'll bring this.'

The sun was beautifully warm at this hour without being overpowering. Seated at the oval table, Lisa enjoyed every mouthful of the meal. She even managed a couple of pieces of toast and marmalade along with the coffee Brett had also insisted on making.

'That's about the most cholesterol I've had at one sitting in years!' she exclaimed with rueful afterthought when the last crumb was finished.

Leaning back in his chair, legs comfortably stretched, Brett gave her an amused glance. 'A little indulgence won't do you any harm. Have some more coffee.'

Lisa shook her head. 'I really have had enough. You're a very good cook.'

'I get by when I need to,' he acknowledged. 'What do you fancy doing today?'

'Anything,' she said expansively. 'Anything at all!'

His smile was slow. 'In that case, how about going sailing again?'

'On *Seajade*, you mean?'

'No, I've a cabin cruiser I keep for my own private use. She's berthed down at the yacht harbour.'

'That sounds great,' she said. 'Shall we be able to snorkel?'

'I'm afraid I only keep scuba equipment on board the *Lindos*, and that takes a deal more training.'

'It doesn't matter,' Lisa disclaimed quickly. 'I'll be happy just to be out there again. I really enjoyed yesterday.'

'So did I.' His tone was soft. 'Particularly certain parts of it.' He watched her colour rise, his smile teasing. 'You blush beautifully.'

'And you enjoy giving me reason to,' she accused.

'True. It's been a long time since I met a woman who still could.'

'It's called a lack of sophistication,' Lisa answered wryly.

'I prefer to call it a delightful change.' He stirred himself, voice briskening. 'Time we made a move.'

Like the rest of the house, the guest bathroom was luxuriously appointed, the shower contained within a separate, glass-fronted cabinet. There was even a hairdrier provided. Lisa used it to good effect, thankful that the smooth styling required nothing more than a brush to set it in order.

Judging from the faint sounds she could hear, Brett was right next door. She wondered what it would be like to share a shower with him—to make love with water cascading all around. She wanted him now, this very moment. If he walked through that door she would be ready for him.

He didn't, of course. He wouldn't be that crude. He was waiting for her when she eventually emerged, tall and vital in white shorts and casual blue shirt. His hair was still damp, the ends slightly curly. Looking at him, Lisa felt that no other man in the world could ever evoke the same response in her.

'I should have worn shorts too,' she said. 'It would only take me a few minutes to go and change.'

'You're fine as you are,' Brett assured her easily. 'You can always put your bikini back on once it's dry. I rang down and asked for the boat to be provisioned from the restaurant, so we'll have lunch on board.'

They left in the Ferrari via a winding road which came out close by the yacht harbour. The *Lindos* was a sleek white thirty feet of sea-going elegance. Worth a fair-sized fortune in itself, judged Lisa bemusedly, watching Brett start up the engines. She hadn't really thought all that much about it before, but he had to be in the millionaire category.

So it was only money, she reflected. It was Brett himself she was drawn to, not his wealth. At the same time, it had to make a difference. The women he was used to being with would take all this for granted, not sit gawping like overawed schoolgirls.

He took the boat well clear of the harbour before sparing her a glance, starting her pulses racing with the intimate quality of his smile.

'My favourite environment,' he said. 'I've a feeling it could be yours too.'

Lisa laughed and lifted her shoulders. 'I'll let you know at the end of the day.'

His gaze roved her wind-swept hair and tanned face, lingering on the curve of her mouth. 'I can tell you now. You're a natural. Stay exactly the way you are—temper and all.' The last was said with a grin. 'Not that I've seen so much of it today.'

'Probably because you haven't done or said anything to provoke it,' she returned. 'Anyway, it's about time I learned to control it more.'

'Pity,' he said. 'I enjoy our spats.'

'As a novelty?'

He grinned again. 'Meaning I'm more accustomed to having a woman agree with me? There could be something in that.'

'Including Andrea Gordon?'

The grey eyes gave little away. 'Andrea has a mind of her own.'

'I'm sure she has.' Lisa would have given anything to retract the question. 'She seems very sure of herself,' she floundered.

'That's the way she is. We may get to see the *Atlantis* coming up in a little while,' he added.

Lisa seized gratefully on the change of subject, aware of having made a gaffe. Brett's relationship with Andrea was not open for discussion; he couldn't have made that clearer.

'The *Atlantis*?' she queried.

'A custom-built submarine designed for viewing the reefs at close quarters without getting wet. It can go down a hundred and fifty feet. Forty-six passengers a trip, plus a crew of three. Safe as houses too. All the systems are duplicated. Great value for those who'd never get to see a reef otherwise.'

Probably the only way she would have got to see one herself if Richard hadn't invited her to accompany him yesterday, Lisa reflected. At the very least, she had that experience to look back on.

And the rest of today to look forward to, she tagged on determinedly. No matter what the consequences.

'I forgot to phone home!' she exclaimed on a rueful note, suddenly remembering. 'Mum will be imagining all sorts of things gone wrong!'

Brett smiled. 'Mothers are like that. Mine certainly was.'

'Was?' Lisa queried softly.

'She died several years ago.'

'I'm sorry. And your father?'

'He married again.' His tone discouraged further enquiry. 'What does yours do?'

She answered with some slight reluctance. 'He's a vicar.'

Brett gave her a swift sideways glance. 'Why so defensive?'

He was too perceptive by half, she thought wryly. She lifted her shoulders. 'It's just that I usually get some funny remark or other about vicars' daughters.'

'And you expected no better from me.' He shook his head. 'I see nothing even remotely risible in your being a vicar's daughter. How did your parents feel about you coming all the way out here?'

'They'd naturally prefer me to be closer to home, but they thought it a fine opportunity to see a little more of the world.'

'Then they wouldn't be too cut up if you stayed?'

'I don't imagine so.' It was Lisa's turn to slant him a glance. 'Are you still going to make me wait out the whole six weeks?'

'As I said yesterday, don't make the job an issue,' came the smooth response. 'Your suit should be dry by now if you want to change.'

Lisa pressed no further. Brett's refusal to be tied down was hardly encouraging, but she wasn't about to dwell on it. What would be would be.

Tied to the aft rail to blow in the wind, her bikini was quite dry. She went down to the cabin to put it on, emerging again to find that Brett had taken advantage of her absence to strip down to trunks himself. They were coming up on one of the smaller, uninhabited islands, little more than a beach backed by palm trees.

'I thought we might anchor here and have a swim before we eat lunch,' he said.

Emboldened by her earlier success, Lisa risked a dive from the side of the boat into the crystal-clear water when the moment came, rather than suffer the indignity of jumping feet first. Brett followed suit, but made no attempt to touch her this time, seemingly content to swim alongside her.

'Don't overdo it,' he warned when she attempted to increase her pace. 'I shouldn't need to tell you how easy it is to strain muscles you're not all that accustomed to using. You can use the pool to build up gradually.'

Lisa had ached the previous night after the day's exertions, and knew she would probably do so again tonight, but Brett was right about trying to improve her performance too quickly. The last thing she needed was an injury.

They ate lunch on deck, choosing from a selection of cold cuts, salads, crusty breads, cheeses and fresh fruit that would have fed a small army. Sun-warmed, the smooth red wine they washed it all down with was delicious. The only cloud on Lisa's horizon at present was the reminder of Brett's departure.

'What time will you be leaving tomorrow?' she was moved to ask at last.

'Early,' he said, dispatching the faint hope that it wasn't true. 'I've a meeting scheduled at three.'

They were reclining side by side on the padded mattresses laid out on the upper deck, shielded from the full force of the sun by a light canopy. Lisa searched her mind for something to add. 'It's going to be a rush,' was all she could come up with.

'I'll make it. I'll be gone all week, but I should make it back here for the weekend.'

Her heart leapt, but caution still held sway. 'You people think nothing of hopping on a plane,' she said lightly. 'Like catching a bus!'

'*We* people?' His tone was quizzical.

'Americans. I know you're not one, but you have the same kind of outlook.'

'As a matter of fact, I was naturalised years ago,' he said. 'Does it make any difference?'

To what? Lisa wondered. 'After all this time out here, I'd have thought you'd have lost your English accent altogether,' she commented, side-stepping the question.

'It isn't an easy thing to lose. Not that I'd want to anyway.' He stretched lazily, grimaced and rubbed the back of his shoulder. 'Seems I might not be quite as fit as I thought.'

'Anyone, no matter how fit, can pull the occasional muscle,' she said on a practical note. 'You only have to consider professional athletes. Would you like me to ease it for you?'

'Sounds a good idea.' He rolled over on to his stomach, head turned away from her, arms relaxed. 'I put myself in your capable hands.'

Lisa willed herself to be objective about it as she began work on the shoulder, but her will-power was hardly equal to the task. The smooth, supple feel of him stirred her senses to a point where professionalism went right out the window.

'Any better?' she asked huskily at length.

'Some,' Brett returned without lifting his head. 'Don't stop there. Give me the full works—the way you did last time.'

Lisa was only too willing to carry on. Over the following moments, she lost herself in sheer tensile pleasure. His body was so magnificently structured, the proportions perfect for his height. She lingered lovingly over each and every muscle group, hearing his roughened breathing through the heavy pounding of her heart. It was going to happen, just as she had known it would. What Brett Sanderson wanted he made sure he got. Well, that was OK, because it was what she wanted too. So much so that her whole body yearned for his touch.

When he turned over on to his back, it was obvious at once that he was on the same wavelength. He reached for her hungrily, cradling her face between his hands as he kissed her with a passion that elicited an instant and unbridled response. Lying along the length of his body, she could feel the throbbing tumescence of his arousal against her thigh, and moved instinctively to fit herself more closely to him, tremoring as his hands slid down the length of her back and under the band of her bikini bottom to cup her buttocks and bring her even closer.

The sensation was exquisite. Lisa moaned deep in her throat, burying her face in the wiry curl of hair on his chest as she had wanted to do so badly the previous day, tasting the salt on her lips as she kissed his taut, damp skin. The musky male scent of him stimulated her senses, intensifying the hunger in her. She wanted to be closer still, to have him inside her, filling her with his hardness, satisfying that need she was only just beginning to know in any depth.

His move to turn her under him was purposeful. Dazed with passion, she parted her lips to him without volition when he kissed her again, clinging to him mindlessly as his tongue drove into her. Time ceased to have any meaning. All she knew was the frenzy of feeling his mouth and hands enkindled in her, the total lack of inhibition in her responses, her body moving with unstudied sensuality against him.

'You're beautiful,' he said thickly against her mouth. 'Beautiful, beautiful Lisa!'

He removed the bikini with practised ease, tossing the two scraps of material aside to savour her with his eyes for a moment before lowering his head to her breasts. His tongue was like fire on her tender, aching flesh, his mouth an agony she couldn't bear yet didn't want to stop. She gasped when his hand slid between her legs to find the moist nub, but made no effort to escape the sensitive caress, writhing in mounting abandonment as he penetrated her most intimate self.

His trunks had gone too, she found when she reached for him, though at which point he had removed them she had no idea. The silky hardness of him made her shudder, but in exultation, not dread. He shuddered himself as she caressed him, pulsing beneath her fingers and groaning with pleasure.

Then he was over and above her and she was guiding him into her, wrapping her limbs about him as he drove to the very centre of her being. It felt so right, so very right—as if she had lived her whole life for this one moment.

Which she had. She knew that already. Brett was the only man she wanted, the only man she could ever want.

When he began to move it was slowly, so slowly at first, each thrust long and deep. Lisa moved with him, delighting in her ability to match him, to take him. He filled her as if made for her and her alone, leaving no part of her untouched. Total possession, and utterly wonderful!

The pace quickened as passion mounted. She dug her fingers into his back, hearing the breath rasping in his throat as they pounded together with ever-increasing force and power. A cry was torn from her throat as spasm after delicious spasm rippled through her, followed a moment later by his hoarse answering cry as control was stripped from him by his own flooding climax.

The sun was considerably lower in the sky when the world finally stopped revolving. Lying there, Lisa thought she could never be more fulfilled than she was at present. Making love with Brett was everything she had ever dreamed it might be. More, in fact, because imagination could only go so far.

Richard was right, of course. She was in love with this man, and had been almost from the first. Love wasn't rational. It happened regardless of what common sense dictated.

That it was purely one-sided she was in no doubt. That the affair was likely to fizzle out quickly now he'd had what he wanted she was also in little doubt. She would cope when she had to, but for now she was going to put it to the back of her mind.

'You're a revelation, do you know that?' he said softly, startling her because she had thought him asleep.

'In what way?' she asked equally softly.

'Every way. You hold nothing back.' He came up on an elbow, running his eyes down the length of her body with a reminiscent smile. 'And English women are supposed to be so cold!'

'Only because so many Englishmen are lousy lovers,' she returned lightly.

'The voice of experience?'

'More hearsay.' She kept the same inconsequential tone. 'I don't make a habit of this.'

The grey eyes were quizzical. 'You mean I'm a special case?'

Lisa felt her heart contract; it was an effort to keep the act going. 'Irresistible!'

His hand came up to stroke the hair away from her temple where it clung damply, making her quiver. 'You're all of that yourself.'

'You managed to overcome it the other night,' she reminded him.

'Cutting off my nose to spite my face. I spent the rest of the night kicking myself.'

'That must have been painful.'

'It was. I had to do a whole lot of rearranging to get down again this weekend.' The smile came again. 'But it was worth it.'

'You came because of me?'

'Why else? I only joined the *Seajade* cruise because I saw your name down on the list.'

'But you still brought Andrea along.'

'An unavoidable circumstance.' He regarded her thoughtfully. 'Do I detect a trace of resentment?'

'Hardly.' Lisa was anxious to nullify any such impression. 'I've no reason to resent her.'

'But you don't like her.'

It was a statement rather than a question, but it still called for an answer. 'We don't have a great deal in common.'

'No,' he said, 'I don't suppose you do.' He trailed a feather-light finger down her cheek, lingering to caress the pulse spot at the base of her ear. 'Have you ever been in love?' he asked unexpectedly.

Lisa closed her eyes, the better to concentrate on that sensitive touch. 'I once thought I was.'

'So what changed your mind?'

'I realised I was wrong, that's all.'

'And how did the man in question feel?'

'I think his pride suffered more than his heart.'

'But you can't be sure.'

'Well, no, I don't suppose I can.' The finger had moved on down the length of her throat to circle her breast, creating havoc with her pulse-rate. 'It was more than a year ago.'

'And there's been no one else since?'

'No one important to me.' She waited a couple of heartbeats before allowing herself to ask the same question. 'How about you?'

'Not in any depth.' There was no element of regret in the statement.

'I suppose that's why you aren't married,' she said on what she hoped was a neutral note.

'It takes more than love to make a marriage work out.'

'But it is an essential element.'

'Desirable. I always considered compatibility more important.'

'Isn't it the same thing?'

'Too many make that mistake, and finish up in the divorce courts. If and when I take a wife, I don't intend that to happen.'

Was this a subtle way of damping down any hopes she might be entertaining? wondered Lisa hollowly. If so, he needn't bother.

'I'm sure you won't make any mistakes,' she said. She pressed herself upright, eyes seeking the discarded bikini. 'Isn't it time we started back?'

'Not yet,' Brett said roughly, and pulled her down again, rolling on top of her to pin her beneath him. 'We only just got started.'

Gazing into the grey eyes, feeling the renewal of passion in his body and her own surging response, Lisa was only too willing to submit. Whatever the price eventually to be paid, the here and now was more important to her.

They made harbour just before sunset. Driving up the hill, with the whole panorama spread beneath a flame-red sky, Lisa fought to stay on top of her emotions. The coming week was going to be difficult to get through. Much as she loved her job, it held little interest at present.

Considering the limitations of their relationship, it might be a good idea if she upped and left St Thomas on her own initiative, she reflected, difficult though it would be. She had Brett's interest now, but how long would it last? Once he did lose interest, he might consider it expedient to send her packing anyway. That would explain his reluctance to commit himself to any contract.

'You look very pensive,' he commented, glancing her way. 'Tired?'

Lisa forced a smile, a shake of her head. 'I was just thinking.'

He returned the smile, eyes enigmatic. 'It's been quite a day. What about dinner? We could go out somewhere.'

Caution fought a brief battle with temptation, and lost. Take what she could of him while she could; wasn't that what she'd said?

'I'll need to change,' she murmured.

'Naturally,' he said drily. 'So will I. I'll drop you off at the main gates and pick you up again at eight. Time enough?'

'Plenty.' Lisa would have preferred to spend the evening up at the house on their own, but wasn't about to say so. There was always the chance that he would take her back there later for a nightcap.

Shameless! she admonished herself, but it did no good.

The bats were beginning to swoop as she went up the drive in the scented dusk. So far she had found little in the way of insects, even at night, but they were obviously there in the air. Looking out over the familiar scene spread below, she knew she could have been totally happy here in other circumstances. Falling in love with Brett was the biggest mistake of her life.

CHAPTER EIGHT

MISTAKE or not, Lisa dressed for the evening ahead with anticipation, choosing a slim-skirted, dark red dress with a scooped neckline and no sleeves, and stepping into matching high-heeled sandals. The night was warm enough to go without a wrap, but she took along a soft white stole just in case.

Finding Brett waiting for her with the car out front was something of a shock.

'I thought you were going to pick me up at the gates?' she said, conscious of eyes on the pair of them as he put her into the passenger seat.

'Reluctant to be seen with me?' he asked with faint irony.

'I was thinking more from your point of view,' she defended.

'As I already told you, my business is my business.' He closed the door, looking down at her for a moment without moving. 'Are you prepared to follow the same line?'

'Yes,' she said recklessly.

His smile was an encouragement in itself. 'Good.'

He came round the front to slide in beside her and start the engine with a flick of a lean brown wrist. The humidity level was higher than normal tonight, Lisa judged, glad of the breeze through her hair as they headed down the floodlit drive.

'What does it feel like to own a place like the Royale?' she asked impulsively, and wished she hadn't as she felt his surprised glance.

'No different from any other place, I suppose.'

'But you must be proud of its success,' she insisted.

'If there's been any doubt, I'd never have contemplated it.' His tone was matter-of-fact. 'The site was right, the time was right, and I liked the idea of having a base down here in addition. Boston's a good place to live, but the weather can be pretty lousy at times—especially in winter. You've never been there?'

'I've never been this side of the Atlantic before,' she acknowledged. 'I've always spent holidays in Europe.'

'Culture tours?'

She laughed. 'Not wholly. I go skiing in the winter.'

They had turned out on to the coastal road. Brett slammed on the brakes as the vehicle in front suddenly pulled up, steering round it without comment and with no visible perturbation. For the first time it dawned on Lisa that, unlike most other cars here, this one was right-hand drive, making overtaking so much safer. All the same, he was being remarkably cool about the near-miss.

'Does anyone here ever bother looking in their driving mirror?' she ventured.

'If they do it makes little difference. I had this shipped out so I could at least see what was coming the other way.' He changed gear for the sharp corner coming up, then again as they headed up the steep hill beyond. 'We have excellent skiing country within easy reach of Boston,' he added. 'You should try it.'

Hardly an invitation, reflected Lisa wistfully. He was simply making conversation. 'It's not very likely,' she said on as casual a note as she could manage, 'but I'll bear it in mind.'

Brett was silent for several minutes after that. Stealing a glance at the lean profile, she hoped he wasn't bored already. She searched her mind for some topic that might interest him, but came up blank.

'Where are we going?' she asked in desperation.

'A little place I know where the food is good, the atmosphere authentic and the owner a good friend.' There was nothing to be gleaned from his tone. 'I think you'll like it.'

If you do, I know I will, she wanted to answer, but didn't for fear of appearing over-eager to please. 'Sounds interesting,' she said instead. 'You use it regularly?'

'Whenever I'm down. I find it relaxing to mix with the locals.'

Lisa wished she could relax. A few short hours ago she had lain in this man's arms, known the intimate intrusion of his body. There had been no constraint between them then, so why now?

She knew why, of course. Making love with a man like Brett was an all-consuming affair—no past, no future, just the overwhelmingly wonderful present. If she wanted to enjoy what time was left she had to forget about what might or might not be and settle for what was.

The restaurant, if it could truly be called that, stood alone at the junction of two narrow roads. Little larger than a shack, and containing no more than half a dozen tables, only two of which were occupied at present, it had a long wooden bar at one end, with several casually clad men leaning on it, glasses to hand. The bartender was Brett's height but more than twice his girth, chest and arms straining at the seams of his T-shirt. His face broke into a dazzling smile when he saw the newcomers.

''Bout time you brought a lady fren' along!' he boomed. 'What yuh havin'?'

Brett grinned back. 'A couple of yellow birds for starters. Lisa, meet Moses Livingstone Johnson.'

The latter extended a hand as big as a ham across the bar. 'Any fren' of Brett's is a fren' of mine!' he declared benevolently. 'Put it there, li'l lady.'

Lisa did so somewhat tentatively, relieved to get it back in one piece after being shaken with such gusto. The other men shifted up to make room, one of them pushing forward a high stool for her to perch on. All regulars, she gathered as Brett performed more introductions, and none of them showing any resentment at having a woman thrust into their midst, the way a similar, all-male group back home might have done.

'You eatin' tonight?' asked Moses, placing two tall iced glasses filled with a creamy yellow concoction on the bar.

'Where else?' said Brett.

'Then yuh better say what yuh wantin' before we get busy. The *kallaloo's* pretty good.'

'A kind of fish stew with pork,' Brett translated for Lisa's benefit. 'One of my favourites.'

'Then I'm sure to enjoy it too,' she said, poker-faced.

'Try your drink first,' he suggested with an answering glint in his eyes.

She did so, finding it delicious. A heady euphoria took hold of her. This was going to be a good night!

It was too. As Moses had warned, the place soon filled up. With everyone seemingly knowing everyone else, conversations were general for the most part. Lisa had difficulty with some of the phraseology, but loved the gregarious atmosphere.

Brett was completely at home. Listening to him exchanging banter with Moses, hearing his hearty masculine laugh ring out, she felt swamped with love for him. The first time he'd turned up with a lady friend in tow, according to what Moses had said. That gave her a great deal of pleasure. Andrea wouldn't fit in for certain. She would turn up her nose at bare wooden floors and pink plaster walls, no matter how spotlessly clean.

It was midnight before she knew it. Even then they were the first to leave, with Brett claiming an early departure the next morning as the reason for breaking things up when, as Moses said, they'd 'only jus' got goin'.

'So how was it?' he said in the car.

Lisa slid both hands around her nape to lift the hair from the back of her neck, only now beginning to come down from her high.

'Absolutely wonderful!' she declared, trying to retain the mood for as long as possible. 'I don't think I've ever enjoyed myself as much!'

His lips slanted. 'I'm not sure I appreciate that remark.'

Not about to try pretending that she didn't know what he meant, she shook her head. 'Hardly the same thing. This afternoon was...'

'Was what?' he prompted when she failed to complete the sentence.

'Something special,' she finished in defiance of the caution taking over again.

'I'm glad to hear it. I'd hate to think I was the only one who thought so.' His tone was level, but with an underlying note that set her heart beating faster. '*You're* special too, Lisa. The only woman I've ever felt able to take up there with me.'

'I'm flattered.' It was all she could find to say.

'I'm not trying to flatter you.' He drew in to the roadside, resting an arm along the wheel as he looked at her. 'It's too bad that I have to leave, but I'll be back ASAP. The question is, are you going to be of the same mind when I do get back?'

It was too dark here under the trees to read anything from his eyes, and his voice gave little of his inner thoughts and feelings away either. The question itself was ambiguous.

'Why would I have changed it?' she prevaricated.

'It happens.' Brett put out a hand and drew her to him, searching her face with a narrowed intensity for a moment before dropping his head to find her mouth with his.

Her response was instant, her body moving instinctively into closer contact even as her mind cautioned her against reading too much into what he said. Not wanting to finish things between them right away was a long way from feeling the way she felt. All the same, it was more than she had allowed herself to hope for.

He put her from him with unconcealed reluctance. 'We'd better get back. I need to be alert tomorrow.'

She didn't want to go back. Not, at least, to her own lonely room, and it was obvious that he wouldn't be taking her to the house. A matter of priorities, she thought disconsolately. Business before pleasure. An attitude she should cultivate herself.

He took her all the way up the drive, but made no attempt to kiss her again before letting her out of the car.

'See you,' he said. 'Be good!'

She had little chance of being anything else, reflected Lisa wryly as he pulled away. It was going to be the longest week of her life.

It was certainly one of the busiest. Apart from the hotel clientele, she had people ringing from outside to ask for appointments too, recommended by Felicity Deardon who was attending regularly.

The woman herself had proved easier to get along with than Lisa had anticipated, considering she was one of Andrea Gordon's set. Her husband was a lot older than she, and retired in most senses of the word, from what Lisa gathered, leaving her to her own devices much of the time.

'I'm not saying I hate it here,' she confided during her Wednesday morning session, 'but sun and scenery aren't everything. You've got the best of it, having this to keep you from getting bored.'

'A lot of people would consider you the lucky one, not having to work for a living,' returned Lisa mildly. 'You can do what you like, when you like.'

'Always providing there's something worth doing—and someone to do it with.'

'What about Andrea Gordon?' Lisa suggested. 'She obviously spends a lot of time here.'

'Not exactly what I had in mind, honey,' came the dry reply. 'Anyway, Andrea wouldn't give me the time of day.'

'She invites you to her parties.'

'We make up numbers. So far as Andrea's concerned, there's only one person worth cultivating and that's Brett Sanderson. Not that I blame her. He's all man!' The pause was weighted. 'Wouldn't you say so?'

Lisa kept her voice under strict control. 'I wouldn't know.'

'Oh, come on! Everybody knows about you two. It's a small island, honey. There's nothing gets by. Rumour has it you ditched Gary Conway when Brett came on the scene.'

'Then rumour has it wrong,' said Lisa flatly. 'I'm here on a purely professional basis.'

'You can deny it all you like, it won't convince anybody. Personally, I'm all admiration. Brett's no pushover. You've got the looks, of course, but so have a lot of others he never showed any interest in. How did you manage it?'

'I think this whole conversation has gone far enough,' Lisa stated. 'Your time is up, in any case.'

'Pity.' Felicity wasn't in the least disturbed by the abrupt termination. She sat up, her regard faintly malicious. 'It won't last, you know.'

Lisa made no reply, relieved when the older woman took herself off to the changing-room without further comment. Having her name bandied about the way Felicity had intimated was no joke, but it was a little too late to start worrying about it. If Brett didn't care what people were saying, then she wasn't going to allow herself to pay any heed either.

Brett apart, Richard was the only companion she wanted. She spent most evenings with him.

'I can't understand why Brett's still insisting on the full six weeks' trial,' he declared over dinner. 'You've already proved your worth.' He eyed her reflectively across the lamplit table. 'Have you heard from him?'

Lisa kept her tone level. 'I didn't expect to.'

'After spending all Sunday together?' He was obviously sceptical.

Her shrug was meant to convey indifference. 'You know what they say—out of sight, out of mind.'

'But not with you. Don't try to pull the wool over my eyes, Lisa. You're in love with the guy.'

'It isn't a problem,' she said, abandoning her aloof stance. 'I can handle it.'

'Can you?' he asked softly.

She did her best to infuse certainty into her voice. 'Yes.'

'I think you're kidding yourself. You're nowhere near hard enough just to walk away from it if it does peter out.'

'There's no "if" about it,' she said. 'I'm under no illusions. If Brett does come back again this weekend, it won't be because he can't live without me.'

'How can you be so sure of his feelings? Has he laid it on the line to you?'

'Not in so many words perhaps, but refusing to confirm my appointment is a good enough indication, wouldn't you say?'

Richard looked at her sharply. 'You're saying he intends getting rid of you when the six weeks are up? I can't believe he'd be that calculating.'

Her shrug was brief. 'I don't want to believe it either, but why else would he be so adamant about seeing it through? It could be a problem having me stay on.'

'With some women maybe, not you.'

'You've more faith in me than he probably has.'

'Then he's no judge of character.'

'It isn't my character he's interested in.' Meeting Richard's steady gaze, Lisa felt herself colour a little. 'I've only myself to blame. I could have said no.'

'He'd have accepted it?'

'Providing I'd made it clear that I meant it. Brett knows too much about women to be easily deceived.'

'If he classes you with the general run, then he knows nothing at all!'

Lisa had to smile. 'Unfortunately, you and he have very different outlooks.' She hesitated. 'To be honest, I'm not sure I'd stay on even if I were offered a contract.'

'Maybe it'd be easier all round if you didn't.' Richard regarded her contemplatively. 'If it does come to that, would you consider becoming my personal masseuse? It would mean travelling around with me during the winter, of course, but you'd have your own apartment back in Boston, and the freedom to extend your services to other clients, if you wanted to.'

It was obviously a serious proposal. Lisa hardly knew how to answer.

'It's a wonderful offer,' she said at last, 'but I couldn't let you create a job for me, Richard, grateful as I am for the thought.'

'It would be a great deal more than just a job,' he said. 'You'd be giving me the pleasure of your company too. You'd be free to take a trip home any time you wanted, naturally. I'd be the last to want to deprive your family of you.' He shook his head as she made to speak. 'Don't answer now. Just think about it, will you?'

It was the least she could do, Lisa conceded, although there was no possibility of her accepting. Richard saw her as his daughter's replacement, and she wasn't about to take advantage of those feelings.

He changed the subject after that, but it wasn't easy to put aside. He was, Lisa knew, counting on her saying yes when the time came. Scruples aside, there was some temptation, she had to admit. If nothing else, it would help her get over Brett.

Appointments were booked through the service desk and the following day's list handed over each evening.

The sight of Andrea Gordon's name down for Friday at ten gave rise to a certain foreboding.

She arrived promptly, her manner pleasant enough on the surface but lacking any real warmth. Having already seen her stripped, or just about, Lisa already knew she was in excellent shape. Normally she would have taken a professional pleasure in working on such a body, but today she found difficulty in keeping her mind focused on what she was doing.

Eyes closed, face composed, Andrea made no effort at conversation. When she did finally speak it was straight to the point.

'I'm not attempting to put a stop to whatever you and Brett have going, but I think it only fair to warn you that it's only temporary.'

Lisa froze, unable for the moment to find her voice. 'Is it really any of your business?' she got out at last.

'Oh, I'd say so.' Andrea still hadn't opened her eyes. 'Brett and I have a long-standing arrangement, you see. One we're neither of us quite ready as yet to put into effect. Until we are, we're both free to indulge other interests. I've no objection to him having an affair with you, just so long as you know the situation and don't finish up getting hurt.'

The words formed themselves, born of some deep-seated need to salvage what was left of her pride. 'Grateful as I am for the thought, you needn't concern yourself about that. I've no intention of getting hurt.'

'Fine, then we'll say no more about it.' Andrea gave a contented sigh. 'Felicity was right—you're very good. I may even book another session some time.'

With fifteen minutes of this one still to go, Lisa could only grit her teeth and carry on, trying desperately to empty her mind of everything but the job in hand. It was impossible, of course. The words were emblazoned across it. 'A long-standing arrangement . . . we're both free to indulge other interests'. A freedom they both used to full advantage, no doubt.

Not that that was any consolation. With how many others had Brett exercised that same freedom? she wondered numbly. How many were on hold back in Boston?

The numbness gave way to white-hot rage as the full realisation took hold. How amused he must have been at the ease with which he had reeled her in. His rejection that first night had merely been part of the game; she could see that now. Deprivation increased desire. It was probably true that he wouldn't normally have spent another weekend down here so soon if it hadn't been for her, but he had made sure he didn't go unrewarded for his trouble.

She completed the session without inflicting any damage on her client, although her hands itched to wring the lovely neck. Andrea was in no way concerned with her feelings, only with making sure that she knew exactly where she stood. How any woman—or man either— could accede to that kind of arrangement was beyond belief! The two of them deserved each other.

Andrea gave her an appraising look when she got to her feet. 'I really had you all wrong,' she remarked. 'It just goes to show how false impressions can be.'

'Doesn't it?' Lisa answered tonelessly. 'Have a nice day.'

The stuffing went out of her once the other woman had departed. She had a free period before her next client, much to her relief. What she needed was time to think, to decide how she was going to handle this situation.

Despite what he had said on Sunday night, there was every possibility that Brett wouldn't bother returning this weekend. By the time he did put in an appearance she had to be sufficiently in control of her emotions to show him exactly where to get off. It wouldn't be easy, but it was essential that he never guess the extent of her involvement. His only weak spot was his masculine pride. That was where she would hit him. If it resulted in her losing any chance of retaining her position here, then so be it. She would be better off back home among people she could trust.

The day dragged in a way it had never done before. Lisa had to concentrate her mind in order not to defraud her clients. So many people liked to chat while they were undergoing treatment. She found it difficult to carry on a conversation as if nothing had happened.

Preparing for her final appointment of the day, she thought of the evening stretching ahead with mounting depression. Richard would be more than pleased to have her dine with him again, she knew, but she wasn't yet sufficiently in command of herself to be sure of concealing her state of mind. His opinion of Brett had already undergone modification. This latest development was liable to arouse every protective instinct in him—the way it would have done with his real daughter. The last thing she needed was to have him confront Brett on her behalf, which she believed him quite capable of doing.

Turning round to see Brett himself standing in the outer doorway was such a shock that she could only stare at him. He was wearing a dark grey business suit, which appeared to indicate both a hasty departure and an impatience to see her that precluded an initial visit to the house to change into more suitable clothing. Before

Andrea's visit she would have found such signs encouraging. Right now, all she felt was sick.

The grey eyes took on a quizzical expression as he registered her lack of welcome. 'I thought I might at least merit a "Nice to see you again",' he said drily. 'Had a hard day?'

'No more than usual.' Her voice sounded as if it was coming from a distance. 'I'm expecting another client any minute.'

He studied her, a faint frown creasing his brow. 'Something wrong?'

The accusation trembled on her lips, but she bit it back. In all probability he wouldn't turn a hair. Her original idea was better. Always providing she could carry it through. Her shrug was brief.

'Nothing of any importance.'

If he didn't believe it, he apparently wasn't inclined to delve any further at the moment. 'Come on up to the house when you're through,' he said. 'We need to talk.'

'I don't really think we have anything very much left to *talk* about.' Lisa kept the emphasis subtle, but knew it hadn't been lost on him as his expression altered.

'That remains to be seen. I'll expect you in an hour.'

He was gone before she could voice any further rebuttal, passing her next client on the way. The woman came in looking arch.

'Our Mr Sanderson is certainly spending a lot of time here lately,' she observed. 'Other years, we've hardly seen him at all. A real dynamo of a man, isn't he?'

'I imagine he has to be in order to keep on top of all his business enterprises,' replied Lisa with a lightness she was far from feeling. 'How's the back today?'

Successfully side-tracked, the woman launched into a detailed report. Lisa listened with only half an ear, the rest of her attention given to contemplation of what she was going to do about Brett. Whereas any other man might take the hint that she didn't want to continue the association, she doubted if he was going to. If she didn't go up to the house as requested, there was every chance that he'd come looking for her.

So go on up there and tell him straight, she counselled herself determinedly. He might not like it, but there was little enough he could do about it.

Be that as it may, she took her time clearing up after her client finally departed. It was almost six o'clock by the time she finished, and more than an hour already since Brett had issued his orders.

She made her way with lagging steps to obey the summons, hardly caring whether anyone saw her going up to the house or not. The sun had set in its usual blaze of glory, but for once she had no interest in the view. All she wanted was to get it over with.

Changed now into white linen trousers and short-sleeved shirt, Brett waited for her as usual on the patio. He watched her approach without stirring from his chair, his expression unreadable.

'I made margaritas,' he said, indicating the covered jug and glasses standing ready on the table. 'Do you like it with or without the salt?'

Lisa had come to a halt a few feet away, hands in the pockets of her tunic. 'Neither, thanks,' she returned with creditable steadiness. 'This isn't a social call.'

Dark brows lifted sardonically. 'Tell me about it.'

She hesitated, not at all sure how to say it now that the moment was on her. 'I didn't expect you back so soon,' she hedged.

'I said ASAP,' came the reply. 'Made other arrangements, have you?'

Her chin firmed. 'What would you expect?'

'Obviously more than you seem inclined to allow me.' He added abruptly, 'Who are you seeing? Hanson?'

'Yes.' Richard would back her if asked, Lisa knew. 'We're going to St Croix tomorrow,' she improvised. 'Perhaps staying overnight.'

'Tell him you can't go.'

The anger was as much a defence as a rebuttal. 'I most certainly will not! Who do you think you are?'

'I know who *I* am,' he said. 'What I'm beginning to wonder about again is you.' The grey eyes were narrowed, his mouth hard. 'I thought you were above this kind of game-playing, Lisa.'

'It's no game.'

'Then what?'

She drew in a shallow breath, forcing herself to hold his gaze. 'One swallow doesn't make a summer.'

His lip curled. 'Supposing you say what you mean without the banalities?'

This time the breath was both deeper- and slower-drawn. 'All right, so I lost interest. Is that plain enough for you?'

'Interest in what exactly?'

'You know very well what I'm talking about.'

'No,' he said, 'I need it underlining for me.'

He was doing this deliberately, Lisa reflected, seeing the steely glint in his eyes. If he wanted it that way then he would have it!

'I mean that once curiosity has been satisfied there's nothing to be gained from repeating an experiment,' she said baldly.

Brett's expression didn't alter. 'That wasn't the impression I gained on Sunday. If I'd asked you, you'd have spent the night with me.'

The sheer arrogance of it took her breath altogether for a moment. She had to fight to control her spiralling temper.

'If it bolsters your ego to believe that, then carry on,' she got out through stiff lips. 'I wouldn't attempt to argue with you.'

She was halfway back to the steps when his hand fell on her shoulder, whipping her round to face him. She hadn't heard him move, and was shocked both by the speed with which he had reached her and the dangerous look in his tautly drawn features. He didn't speak, just pulled her to him to find her mouth with a savagery that paralysed her.

The hardness of his hands when he pushed her abruptly away from him again was almost as painful. A look of self-disgust had replaced the anger in his eyes. He turned without a word and strode away from her, disappearing indoors.

Lisa stood there gazing after him with a heart as heavy as lead. She had achieved what she had wanted to achieve, but it gave her little satisfaction. No matter how illogical, she still loved the man.

CHAPTER NINE

THERE had been no definite arrangement with Richard for that evening, just the intimation that he would be available if required. Lisa was reluctant to phone him, though there was little alternative if she was to lend substance to the claim that they were to visit St Croix tomorrow. He would be willing enough to take her, she was sure, but he would know Brett was back and would naturally be curious as to why she wanted to get away from the Royale.

It came down to a simple choice in the end. Either she told Richard the whole sordid little story, or she ran the risk of having Brett see him around and realise she had been lying about the trip—and, if that, perhaps lying about other things too. Rather the first than the second, she decided.

Richard asked no questions over the phone, but simply said he would have a taxi waiting in half an hour. He didn't say where they would be going, and Lisa didn't care, providing it was somewhere other than here.

Determined not to let her emotional problems take over completely, she made an effort with her appearance. Selina was coming up the stairs as she descended.

'Going out or staying in?' asked the other girl blandly.

The innuendo was all too obvious. News of Brett's return would have gone round the hotel like lightning. Lisa kept her tone casual.

'Going out, as a matter of fact. With Richard Hanson.'

'Oh?' Selina looked nonplussed. 'I'd have thought you'd be seeing the boss tonight. You were up there earlier.' Her expression altered in sudden comprehension. 'He's given you the push, hasn't he?'

'Not at all,' Lisa answered in deliberate misunderstanding. 'I still have three weeks of my trial period to run.' She gave the girl a smile. 'Have a nice weekend.'

The prevarication wouldn't do any good, of course, she reflected wryly, carrying on down the stairs. Selina would lose no time in spreading the word around. It would be galling to have them all believing that Brett had indeed cast her aside, but there was nothing to be done about it. Least said, soonest forgotten, as her mother always maintained.

Richard was waiting as promised with a taxi standing by. He greeted her warmly as usual, and made no reference to Brett at all during the journey across the island to yet another luxury hotel.

'You're spoiling me for ordinary fare,' Lisa protested lightly when they were seated in the opulent gourmet restaurant. 'I've never eaten so well as in these past couple of weeks!'

'You could eat this way all the time if you accept my invitation,' Richard answered. 'Did you give it any serious thought as yet?'

She shook her head, avoiding his gaze. 'I'm not ready to make any major decisions.'

'Too much else on your mind?' His tone was gentle. 'This is the third weekend running that Brett's been down. If you're the reason, why aren't you with him now?'

'Because I prefer to be here with you,' she said.

He smiled. 'I appreciate the compliment, but doubt it's the entire truth. Didn't he contact you at all?'

'Yes, he did.' Lisa gave a rueful shrug. 'He's not the man you thought he was, Richard. If it comes to that, he's not even the man *I* thought he was.'

'So tell me about it,' he invited.

She did so, sticking to the bare facts. He listened in growing anger and indignation.

'I knew he had something of a reputation where women are concerned, but I never imagined him the type to sink as low as that!' he ejaculated when she finished. 'Andrea's as bad. I'd be willing to bet her grandfather doesn't know about this arrangement. A real old Bostonian is Howard. He'd cut her off without a nickel if he ever found out she wasn't Snow White.'

'You're not thinking of telling him?' Lisa queried swiftly.

The hesitation was brief. 'I guess not. I'd hate to be the one to disillusion him. Brett's another matter. He needs a few home truths!'

'I don't want you saying anything to him either,' she asserted, panicking. 'Please, Richard!'

'Why not?' he asked. 'If your father were here, I'm sure he'd do the same.'

'No, he wouldn't, because I'd never have told him about it in the first place.'

'You don't confide in him?'

'He's a vicar, and just as strait-laced as Andrea's grandfather. Both he and my mother would be devastated if they knew I'd been ... on intimate terms with a man outside of marriage.'

'Maybe they're more *au fait* with the modern world than you think.'

'No way.' Lisa could say it with certainty. 'Dad regards promiscuity as the greatest sin of all.'

'You're hardly promiscuous.'

'In his eyes there'd be little difference.' She added quickly, 'I'm not complaining about him—about either of them. It's just the way they are.'

'With your brothers too?'

'Oh, yes. David's married, so he's licensed, but Philip still gets the third degree whenever he's home.'

'Totally without foundation, of course?'

Lisa had to smile. 'I doubt it.'

The arrival of the langoustines comprising their first course took up the next few minutes. Richard waited until the waiter had gone before returning to the more painful subject.

'Everything considered, I imagine there's a chance that Brett might feel inclined to terminate your employment right away.'

Lisa could imagine it too. She could also sense what might be coming next. 'In which case,' she said, 'I'll be spending Christmas back home.'

'Telling your parents what?'

'They'd be happy to believe homesickness.'

'And, once there, it's unlikely you'd be coming back.' It was more statement than question, his tone wry.

'It would never work out,' said Lisa gently. 'No matter how we handled things, people would get the wrong idea.'

'Would that matter so much, providing we knew the truth?'

'It would to me. And to your son too, I should imagine.'

Richard smiled faintly. 'In other words, I'm thinking only of myself.' He shook his head as she opened her mouth to repudiate the suggestion. 'You're probably right at that. I can't expect you to replace Helen simply because I want it. You have your own life to live.'

Not, at present, a very enticing prospect, Lisa was bound to acknowledge. She had no job back in England, and little enough means of support while she looked for one, which meant falling back on her parents for a time. They would be only too ready to have her living at home again, but it would be difficult to adjust after several years of freedom to please herself.

She was looking entirely on the black side, she comforted herself at that juncture. Brett might yet prove big enough to set the whole episode aside in the interests of his clientele. If he did see fit to let her stay on, she could do no less than make the same effort to let bygones be bygones. If...

Disappointed though he obviously was over her decision, Richard proved ready enough to accompany her the following day. Having already declared herself concerned about what people might think, Lisa made no mention of staying overnight. She was hardly likely to see Brett on Sunday unless he went out of his way to seek her out. Notice to quit, should it come to that, would no doubt be channelled through Gary Conway.

More than twice the size of St Thomas, St Croix was dotted with the ruins of sugar mills and great houses. The landscape was much more varied than St Thomas, Lisa found, ranging from arid, cacti-covered areas through to a dense rainforest with giant mahogany trees overhanging the narrow, winding roadway. Flowers bloomed everywhere in a riot of colour. The flamboyant red of the poinsettia was a sharp reminder of how close they were to Christmas.

'You should see the British Islands too,' said Richard on the plane going back to St Thomas. 'Virgin Gorda is supposedly just about crime-free. We could go Christmas week if——'

'If I'm still here,' Lisa finished for him.

'I was going to say if you'd like to,' he returned. 'To be honest, I'd forgotten about the other matter for the moment.'

Lisa wished she could forget it too. It had been sleeting in Northwood when she had phoned home before leaving that morning. Her mother had sounded unusually despondent, although she had denied feeling so. Lisa had been tempted to tell her she was coming home, but some stronger force had held the words in check. She would go if pushed; otherwise, she was going to stick it out, she had decided there and then. A job such as this one was surely worth hanging on to, whatever the cost.

She parted from Richard on reaching the hotel, having agreed to meet him later for dinner. Any guilt she felt over using him as an anodyne was alleviated by the knowledge that he took genuine pleasure in her company. Whatever happened with regard to her job here, they would have to say goodbye sooner or later, of course. She would miss him, but the life he had offered her was simply out of the question.

Gary Conway was talking with some guests in the rear courtyard. Lisa felt her heart lurch when he signalled her to wait. There was only one thing he could have to say to her. She steeled herself to take it on the chin.

The smile he donned on taking his leave of the paying guests faded abruptly as he turned to her.

'Seems you won't be seeing very much more of your friend Hanson,' he said without preamble. 'Unfortunately, we're unable to extend his reservation over Christmas. He's scheduled to leave tomorrow.'

Lisa gazed at him blankly for a moment before anger came crashing in on her. 'You can't do that!' she exclaimed.

Gary lifted an eyebrow. 'Sure we can. The suite's needed for incoming guests.'

'He decided he wanted to stay on two weeks ago. You must have known the state of affairs then.'

'He may have decided then, but he didn't bother advising us of his change of plan until this morning,' was the unmoved reply. 'People in his bracket tend to take too much for granted.'

'People in his bracket are usually accorded every possible facility by very virtue of their standing,' Lisa retorted. 'Are you saying you don't even have room in the annexe?'

'I'm saying we can't extend his reservation.'

She looked at him straight and hard. 'Your decision—or Brett's?'

His eyes flickered. 'It's his hotel.'

'And you're just his mouthpiece when it comes right down to it.' She was being unfair and she knew it, but she had to hit out at someone. 'I thought better of you than that, Gary!'

'When it comes right down to it, I'm a paid employee,' came the clipped retort. 'I follow orders. If it were up to me, you'd be the one leaving. You've been nothing but trouble since you got here!'

'Part of it being the fact that I failed to live up to *your* expectations!' Lisa caught herself up, aware of coming close to saying too much. 'I came to do a job I was well-qualified for,' she said in more moderated tones. 'In all fairness, you can hardly say I've failed you there.'

His shrug was dismissive. 'Maybe so, but you're still a load of trouble. Brett must be crazy to risk alienating

someone like Hanson just because he has the hots for
you himself. He'll think so too once he's had enough of
you. And that won't be long, you can bet on it!'

Either Selina had seen fit to keep her suppositions to
herself for once, or the grapevine wasn't as efficient as
she had imagined, Lisa reflected. Not that it was important at the moment. What did concern her was the
way Brett had chosen to show her who was really in
charge. Getting rid of Richard was just the beginning.
Her turn was still to come. Only she wasn't going to
hang around waiting for it.

Without another word she turned purposefully away,
leaving Gary standing there. Righteous anger kept her
going all the way to the upper level, faltering a little when
she found the patio empty but coming back in full force
as her eye caught movement inside the house. He was
there all right!

One of the sliding glass doors was already open. She
went in without hesitation, looking with loathing at the
man framed within the rear archway.

'You just can't take it, can you?' she shot at him.

Hands in trouser pockets, one shoulder propped neg-
ligently against the near wall, Brett looked back at her
expressionlessly.

'Take what?'

'Being turned down. The first time ever, was it?'

'The first time with such a lack of finesse, maybe.'
His tone was quite level. 'Is that all you came to say?'

Her blue eyes blazed. 'You know why I'm here! You
obviously don't consider it good business policy to turf
me out this side of Christmas but you're making sure I
don't have anything more to do with Richard Hanson!'

'Something like that.' The irony was faint. 'Anything else?'

Lisa almost choked on the bitter rage filling her. 'You're so sure of yourself, aren't you?' she got out. 'The great Brett Sanderson, lord of all he surveys! Short on integrity, but who cares about that these days? You and Andrea are well-suited!'

He straightened abruptly away from the wall. 'Where does Andrea come into it?'

Mentioning the woman's name had been a mistake, Lisa acknowledged ruefully. She was in danger of revealing too much.

'There's no point in any of this,' she declared. 'If Richard leaves tomorrow, then I'm going with him!'

Brett put out a hand as she started to turn, and pressed one of a bank of switches set into the wall close by. Lisa saw the door through which she had come glide silently closed, heard the click of a lock.

'You're not going anywhere,' he stated flatly, 'until you tell me how my supposed lack of integrity relates to Andrea Gordon.'

His use of the woman's full name struck a somewhat incongruous note, though hardly enough to create any doubt. It was too late for prevarication, Lisa accepted fatalistically. She might as well get it over with.

'Anyone agreeing to *that* kind of arrangement has to be lacking in integrity,' she stated. 'Even if the things you've accused me of were true, you'd have no room to talk!'

His frown increased. 'What arrangement?'

'Oh, don't try denying it, *please*!' Lisa could hardly contain her disgust. 'At least have that much decency!'

'I'm denying nothing until I know what you're talking about,' he said through his teeth. His hands were out of his pockets now, his whole stance tense. '*What* arrangement?'

Lisa gazed at him in sudden uncertainty, brought up short despite herself. If he was acting the part then he had missed his vocation.

'Andrea booked a session with me yesterday,' she said, rallying her resolve. 'She told me everything. I'm sure you neither of you suffers frustration while you're waiting for the time to be right, but that doesn't make it any better.'

'Just what was it she did tell you?' Brett demanded. 'Exactly what she said, not what you might have surmised.'

'I surmised nothing. She was very explicit. But why wait at all? I shouldn't have thought marriage need stop you enjoying the same freedom to indulge yourselves!'

Brett regarded her with an odd expression. 'You believe I plan to marry Andrea at some point?'

'That's what she gave me to understand.' Lisa's lip curled. 'I suppose *you're* going to tell me it isn't true.'

He said without undue emphasis but with a rock-steady gaze, 'I've never discussed marriage with any woman.'

She looked up at him stonily. 'You're saying she made it all up?'

'If it isn't true, then she must have done.'

'*If.* That's the operative word, isn't it? One of you has to be lying!'

'That,' he returned, 'is something you'll have to decide for yourself.'

Lisa hardly knew what to believe. If Brett was telling the truth, then Andrea had simply been trying to break the two of them up. That would mean she regarded her, Lisa, as a threat, which was ridiculous.

'I think we need to get a whole lot of things straight between us,' he said when she failed to respond.

Such as the exact significance of their own relationship, for instance, she assumed. Well, he needn't bother. She knew just where she stood.

'We already did,' she said flatly. 'It's only a side-issue anyway. I'm here because of Richard. He isn't responsible for what I told you last night.'

'Any more than I'm responsible for what Andrea told *you*,' came the dry reply.

'You must have given her *some* cause to believe she had a claim on you,' Lisa protested, drawn despite herself. 'Why else would she have done it?'

Brett shrugged. 'Probably sour grapes. She's accustomed to having what she wants.'

'And she wants you?'

'She considers me a good prospect, yes.'

'I'm sure she isn't on her own in that.'

The sarcasm drew a faint smile. 'Maybe not.' He eyed her reflectively. 'Why didn't you tell me all this last night instead of putting on that act?'

Her chin lifted. 'What makes you so sure it was an act?'

'This,' he said with purpose.

Lisa stood her ground as he came over to her, heart thudding against her ribs. Believing him was difficult enough, resisting him even more so, feeling the way she still did about him. She held herself stiff and unresponsive as he pulled her up to him, her lips tightly closed against the seeking pressure.

Only not for long. Brett saw to that by simply refusing to accept any rejection. Groaning inwardly in recognition of her weakness, she melted against him, arms sliding about his neck, mouth moving under his in fervid response. At the moment it didn't matter what she believed. The physical contact alone was too much to withstand.

She put up no resistance when he slid an arm under the back of her knees and lifted her, burying her face in the curve where his shoulder merged with his neck. The musky masculine scent of him was a stimulant in itself. She brushed aside the collar of his shirt to press her lips to the warm bare skin, loving his strength and vitality and pushing all else to the furthest recesses of her mind.

He carried her along a corridor and down some steps, kicking open a door to stride across a room and set her down on a wide bed. Lisa welcomed him with open arms as he lowered himself to her, fingers curving about the swell of his biceps for a moment before running lightly up and over the muscular breadth of his shoulders to reach the crisp line of hair at his nape. His kisses lit skyrockets in her head and heart. She quivered to the touch of his hand as he slid it beneath the loose cotton top she was wearing.

Her lacy wisp of a brassière was no barrier. A moan broke from her lips as the long, tensile fingers traced infinitely light circles around her aureole. The pain when he brushed her aching, peaking nipple was scarcely bearable yet desirable too. Then the fingers were gone and his mouth was there instead, sucking first softly and then with harder, more demanding pressure, tongue flickering over the very tip like a living flame.

She said his name, voice husky, pleading, wanting more of him. He was fully aroused already; the pulsing hardness sent the muscles of her inner thighs into involuntary spasm. She needed to feel him, to hold him, to know the power in him.

The sun had set long ago, and the room was dark. When he stood up to peel off his clothing he was no more than a shape outlined against the window, tapering from shoulder down to narrow hip. Her own cut-off leggings were removed with dexterity, along with the briefs beneath. Lisa gasped as he slid both hands under her and raised her to his marauding mouth, writhing in a frenzy of sensation.

He worked his way up the whole length of her body, his lips trailing fire across her skin. By the time he reached her mouth she was beyond thinking anything, her abandonment total. She wrapped slender limbs about him as he penetrated her, making no attempt to stifle her cry as he drove all the way to the very centre of her being. They were together again, and nothing else mattered. Together!

It took a long time to come out of that final implosion. Lisa had the feeling that she had actually fallen asleep for a while. Brett was lying on his side, head pillowed on her shoulder, his breath warm on the side of her neck. One arm was thrown across her, hand at her breast. From the even pace of his breathing, he was asleep himself.

Lisa concentrated on the feel of him against her, savouring the memory of their lovemaking. If that first time had been wonderful, this had been even better. She had always believed such ecstasies were reserved only for the very few. Brett had taken her to a place beyond imagining—a place he might well be prepared to take her several times more before his interest in her began to wane.

Reality had to be faced, she acknowledged painfully. This was no more than an affair to him. The kind in which any man of his age and disposition would indulge without a second thought. She was the only one who saw love as a requirement.

One thing was certain—she could hardly, after this, claim a loss of interest on her own behalf, the way she had attempted to do last night. All she could do was attempt to keep him from guessing just how much he really meant to her, and the only way was to pretend that she had never seen it as anything more than an affair either.

She froze as he stirred, then forced herself to relax. The time for retreat was long gone.

'Sorry about that,' he said softly. 'It isn't a habit of mine to fall asleep.' He lifted himself on an elbow to look down at her, mouth pulling into a slow smile. 'You're a pretty exhausting lady!'

Lisa smiled back, lifting a hand to feel the smoothness of his cheek. 'You didn't sleep long enough for this to grow again.'

'I should hope not. That would have been a real waste.' His eyes glinted in the darkness. 'Glad you changed your mind?'

She laughed low down in her throat, wondering at her ability to dissemble this way. 'I'm not sure I ever made it up. I just didn't like being put in that position.'

The smile came again. 'There are others.'

And he would know them all, she thought. Aloud she said, 'I meant by Andrea.'

He studied her, expression veiled. 'You still think we have this arrangement?'

'I think it's immaterial now,' she said. 'After all, there's no commitment between us.'

'So you're prepared to continue our association?'

Lisa put everything she knew into keeping her voice from revealing her inner turbulence. 'While it lasts, why not?'

'Why not indeed?' There was more than a touch of irony in his tone. 'So let's make the most of it while it does last.'

There was less foreplay this time, a certain fierceness in his possession. Lying there nerveless in the aftermath, Lisa wondered if she would ever find anyone else capable of arousing her to the same degree. She had only made love all the way with one other man, and he hadn't managed it. But then she had only thought herself in love with him. Had it been the real thing, it might have been different.

Brett rolled away from her to sit up and reach for the robe draped over the end of the bed. Lisa watched him head for what she assumed was the *en-suite* bathroom, waiting until the door had closed behind him before reluctantly stirring herself.

It took the sight of the illuminated bedside clock to bring her fully to her senses. Almost nine-thirty already, and she had promised to meet Richard at eight! He would have been advised by now of his imminent departure. What would he be thinking?

Her leggings and briefs were on the floor where Brett had tossed them, the cotton top he had removed afterwards down at the foot of the bed. She was struggling into the latter when he came out from the bathroom.

'Leaving?' he asked.

'I didn't realise the time,' she said. 'It was only just gone seven when I came.'

'So we both got carried away for a couple of hours. No reason to run away.'

'I'm not.' She hesitated, uncertain of her ground. 'I was supposed to be having dinner with Richard.'

'You spent all day with him,' came the clipped rejoinder. 'Isn't that enough?'

'If he's to leave tomorrow, I have to say goodbye.'

'But you'd prefer him to stay?'

'Naturally I would. As I already told you, nothing I said last night had anything to do with him. If you want to take it out on anyone, how about Andrea?'

'I'll deal with Andrea in my own time,' he said. 'If Hanson does stay on, are you prepared to stay away from him?'

She bit her lip. 'That's putting me in a cleft stick!'

The shrug was brief. 'Take it or leave it.'

'Why?' she demanded. 'Richard's a friend, nothing more. You can't possibly think we're...'

'Sexually involved?' he supplied as her voice trailed away. 'You may not see him in that light, but I doubt very much if his motives are wholly avuncular. Few men could spend as much time as he has with a beautiful young woman without sexual attraction entering into it at all. And don't bother repeating that piece about his daughter, because I don't go for it.'

'Only because you're a total cynic!' she fired at him. 'You judge everyone by your own standards!'

'And I'm not often wrong.'

'Arrogant, too!' Lisa was incensed, eyes sparking, fists clenched. 'How did I ever let myself get mixed up with someone like you?'

His mouth slanted. 'Are you saying you regret it?'

The mockery spurred her to even greater fury. 'I've never regretted anything more!'

'Liar.' The grey eyes held a glitter of their own. 'You're no more ready to call it a day than I am.'

'That's what you think!'

He was between her and the room door, but she wasn't about to let that stop her. She hit out at him blindly as he took hold of her, hating him with an intensity equal to the passion she had felt earlier.

Brett made no sound, just swung her up in his arms again and carried her back to the bed, slinging her down with a force that jerked the breath from her body and pinning her under him. He was angry himself; she could see that in his eyes. Enough so to stifle any further invective.

His mouth was rough on hers at first, but only until she stopped struggling against him and lay quiescent. Lisa willed herself to stay that way, but it was a losing battle when every instinct in her yearned to answer in kind. She gave in because she couldn't help herself, kissing him back with a kind of desperation.

'Now tell me you want out,' he challenged.

Lying there, looking up into the taut, dark features, she knew a sense of hopelessness. He had her hog-tied.

'It isn't so much a case of wanting out as resenting being told who I can or can't see,' she said, low-toned. 'You don't have the right.'

'I have the right to choose my own clientele.'

'I'm not disputing that, only your reasons for this particular decision.'

'Reasons I'm prepared to stand by.' He wasn't giving an inch. 'As I said, it's your choice.'

She gazed at him impotently. 'Damn you, Brett!'

One dark brow lifted. 'Do I take that as a yes or a no?'

'Yes.' The word was dragged from her by a force stronger than her sense of justice.

Brett made no comment. Levering himself upright, he reached for the telephone at the side of the bed and dialled a number.

'Advise Mr Hanson in suite 113 that there's been a mistake and we can extend his reservation after all,' he said crisply.

'There's a good chance that he'll leave anyway, having already been told to go,' Lisa pointed out as he replaced the receiver.

'His choice,' came the unmoved response. Seated on the edge of the bed, Brett appraised her tousled blonde hair and general dishevelment with a slow smile. 'Hungry?'

Only for you, she could have told him, but it sounded too much like a line from a bad novel. 'A little,' she said instead. 'I haven't eaten since lunch.'

'Then we'd better do something about it. There's plenty of food in the fridge.'

Lisa sat up as he got to his feet, pushing an automatic hand through her hair. 'I've worn these things all day. I need to go and change.'

'No point,' he declared. 'You can take a shower right here, and put on a robe. The bathroom's right over there.'

He was moving as he spoke, heading for the door, the short silk robe belted at his waist outlining a body that Lisa knew now in intimate detail. Just the thought alone was enough to shorten her breath and flutter her stomach muscles.

She wasn't the first woman to know him this way, of course. Even if Andrea was lying about their so-called arrangement, it was odds-on that they had slept together. And not only Andrea either. Brett was a mature and virile man accustomed to freedom of choice. No one woman was going to satisfy him for long.

All the more reason to make hay while the sun still shone for her, she determined. Whatever happened, she would at least have had this much.

The bathroom was enormous by British standards, with a sunken round bath set within a marbled platform. Lisa used the glass shower cabinet, dried herself on one of the thick cream towels, and smoothed a little Versace aftershave over her arms and shoulders before donning the robe hanging ready behind the door. It was far too large for her, of course, both in width and in length, reaching down past mid-calf. On Brett himself it would come to no more than knee-length, she calculated. She liked the feeling of wearing something he had worn.

She found him in the kitchen whipping eggs. He was still wearing the silk dressing-gown, with the leather slippers now on his feet his only addition.

'Spanish omelette and salad OK?' he asked.

'Sounds wonderful,' Lisa agreed. 'Can I do anything?'

'It's all done apart from the omelette,' he returned easily. 'Just sit there and talk to me.'

The breakfast-bar was already laid for two, she saw, with the bowl of salad taking centre place. Perching on one of the high cane stools, she said, 'About what?'

Brett gave her an amused glance. 'Whatever comes to mind. You're not usually stuck fast for a word or two.'

'I'm not exactly accustomed to this kind of situation,' she acknowledged.

He poured the beaten egg into the pan already half full of sizzling vegetables before answering, tone odd, 'You like to keep a man guessing, don't you, Lisa?'

She hesitated. 'I'm not sure what you mean.'

'I mean you're a regular chameleon. You make love like a full-blooded woman then act like some inexperienced girl!'

'I'm not acting anything!' she denied with heat. 'I don't sleep around!'

'If I'd thought that, you wouldn't be here now,' he returned. 'Just stop confusing me, will you?'

'I shouldn't have imagined the word was in your vocabulary!'

'It wasn't much used before I met you, I admit.' He deftly sliced the thick omelette in half, and slid the portions on to the waiting plates, then ditched the pan and brought both plates across to where she sat, his expression unreadable. 'Get it while it's hot.'

Her hunger had passed, but refusing the food now was obviously out of the question. She picked up her fork and dug in as he took the stool opposite, not at all sure of his mood. If she was a chameleon, what was he?

'Don't sulk,' he admonished, bringing her head up sharply.

'I'm *not*——' She stopped short on seeing the glint in the grey eyes, the quirk at the corner of his mouth, a reluctant smile curving her own lips. 'Who's doing the confusing now?'

'So let's be straight on one thing, at any rate,' he said. 'I want to spend the night with you.'

Lisa felt her heart leap, but caution still held sway. 'I'm not sure that's a good idea,' she hedged.

'Meaning you don't want to?'

'That wasn't what I said.'

'Then you do want to?'

She sighed. 'You know I do.'

'I only know what you let me know,' he denied. 'So what's the problem?'

'The talk it's going to cause if I'm seen leaving in the morning, for one thing.'

'We'll make it an early departure, before anyone else is around.'

'There's the night staff.'

'Whom you're unlikely to run into unless you cut right through the lobby.' Brett eyed her uncompromisingly. 'Yes or no?'

She threw caution aside, unable to resist the temptation. 'Yes.'

His laugh was low. 'That's the only answer I was going to accept anyway. Whatever it took.'

The grey eyes were too penetrating by half. Lisa fought to retain what composure she still possessed. 'Do you always win?' she asked lightly.

'Most times. None of us can have everything we want.'

'I don't see you going without very much.'

'Materially, maybe not. There are other things in life.' His glance dropped to her plate. 'You haven't eaten very much. Don't you like it?'

'It's delicious,' she assured him truthfully. 'I'm just not all that hungry after all.'

'Nor me.' He reached across and took the fork from her hand, laying it down along with his own. 'In which case, there seems nothing to stay up for.' His tone roughened. 'I want you, Lisa.'

She said huskily, 'Again?'

'As many times as I can manage.'

He came round the table to draw her to her feet, cupping her face between his hands to kiss her lingeringly, not forcing the pace. Lisa gave herself over to the emotions coursing through her. The night was still young.

CHAPTER TEN

BACK in her own room by sunrise, Lisa found sleep hard to come by. She was fairly confident that she hadn't been seen, despite the lateness of her departure from the house. Brett had wanted her to stay, but it was so easy for him. Everything was easy for him.

The night had been all too short. Lying there, she relived every precious moment of it. Brett was a superb lover. He could also, she had found, be a tender one. There had been a couple of times when she had come dangerously close to saying those three little words that would change everything. He didn't want her love, just her body—and that only on a temporary basis.

She dozed off eventually, awakening at nine feeling anything but refreshed. Brett had said he would phone her, but had mentioned no particular time. If she went for breakfast she might not be here when he did.

Showered, and dressed in a yellow and white cotton wrap-over, she sat down at the dressing-mirror to apply lipstick and run a brush over her hair. Her skin had a soft glow to it, her eyes an added depth. She looked like a woman in love, Lisa reflected, and hoped she was the only one to think so.

The call came at ten. Brett sounded brisk and businesslike.

'Sorry about this, but I have to get back. I'm leaving in five minutes.'

The disappointment was like a knife wound. Lisa struggled to contain it. 'Trouble?'

'Nothing I can't handle, providing I'm there to do it.' The pause was brief. 'I'll see you on Friday.'

Lisa replaced the receiver feeling totally bereft. She had anticipated a whole day with him. Instead she faced a whole week without him. He had sounded so dispassionate too—as if nothing had happened between them. Perhaps, for him, nothing of any great moment had.

No, that couldn't be true, she assured herself. He had gained as much pleasure from their lovemaking as she had. She recalled his voice, roughened with passion— the endearments he had used. Meaningless, perhaps, in the cold light of day, but unfeigned at the time, she was certain.

Friday was the day before Christmas Eve. He hadn't said exactly how long he planned on staying, but Gary had intimated that he usually spent the whole Christmas week. It was a thought to cling to.

In the meantime, she still had today to get through. She hadn't yet visited the underwater observatory over at Coki Point. That should fill a few hours. There was a beach near by, which would take care of a few more. Better, anyway, than hanging round the Royale.

She was almost ready to go before she remembered Richard. Guilt swamped her. Brett had extracted a promise that she would stay away from the older man, but what could she tell him by way of explanation?

It was possible, of course, that the problem had already been solved by Richard's departure, but she doubted if he would have left without some attempt to get in touch.

As if in answer to that thought, the telephone rang again. Lisa briefly contemplated ignoring it, but the certainty of who was calling made that impossible. She went resignedly to lift the receiver.

'What happened?' asked Richard abruptly. 'I was trying all evening to reach you.'

He merited honesty above all, Lisa reflected, difficult though it might be to put across.

'I'm sorry for leaving you standing like that,' she said. 'I...lost track of the time.'

There was silence for a moment. When he spoke again it was on a different note. 'You were with Brett?'

'Yes.'

'What about Andrea?'

'It isn't true what she said. She made the whole thing up.'

'According to Brett?'

'Yes.' Lisa closed mind and heart to any lingering doubt. 'I love him, Richard.'

'And does he love you?'

She lightened her voice. 'He still wants me. That has to be a start. Who knows what might happen?'

'Who indeed?' There was another pause, another change of tone. 'Did you know I'd been refused an extension on my time here?'

Lisa said swiftly, 'There must be some mistake.'

'So it seems. I had a call from the management first thing this morning.'

'And are you going to stay?'

'I've still to decide.' He waited a moment, as if in anticipation of some comment from her, then added levelly, 'Are you spending the day with Brett too?'

'He had to go back. Some business problem to be sorted out before tomorrow. He'll be here over Christmas, though.'

'In that case, what about lunch?'

Lisa hesitated before answering. Brett surely couldn't expect her to ignore the other man completely? Especially when he was so utterly wrong about him. Richard had been so good to her. He deserved better than to be treated that way.

'That would be lovely,' she said.

'One o'clock, then. I'll reserve a terrace table.'

He had rung off before she could protest. Eating here at the Royale was not what she had had in mind. On the other hand, if she was going to go against Brett's edict at all, wasn't it better to be open about it? She had nothing to hide.

The *maître d'* greeted her easily enough when she went over to the restaurant on the hour, taking her out to the terrace where Richard was already seated. The table reserved for management was close by. Gary Conway gave her a curt nod, but offered no verbal greeting.

Looking out over the sparkling, sun-kissed scene, Lisa could hardly believe that it was only three weeks since she had sat here for the first time. She felt a different person.

'You look lovely as usual,' said Richard, appraising the little Italian knit suit she was wearing. 'Did you never consider modelling as a career?'

'When I was about fifteen,' Lisa admitted. 'Along with a few thousand others, I should imagine.' She studied the menu, still not all that interested in food, but needing something on which to concentrate. 'What do you fancy?'

'Something I can't have,' came the steady reply. He smiled as her eyes lifted to his face. 'Don't worry, I'm not about to start trying to persuade you to change your mind. You were right. It would never have worked out.

All I ask for is your company. Naturally, that's only when Brett's not here.'

Lisa gazed at him wretchedly, looking for a way out and finding none. Brett had been wrong to make that demand of her, but she had given her word on it.

'I'm going to be exceptionally busy this week,' she hedged. 'I can see me having to extend my hours. If things go on this way, I'm going to need help.'

Richard's expression had altered, his eyes suddenly shrewd. 'What are you trying to tell me?'

She made an apologetic little gesture. 'I told Brett I'd stay away from you. He's totally wrong, of course, but he won't accept that you only see me as something of a substitute for your daughter. You'll probably think I'm a fool for letting him dictate to me.' She gave a short laugh. 'You'd probably be right at that.'

'Only he's the one you can't say no to.' Richard gave a wry little smile. 'He isn't so wrong, Lisa. Not if I'm honest about it. You're a beautiful, talented young woman, with a heart of pure gold. I'd be a liar if I said my feelings for you were purely platonic.'

'I'm sorry.' She found it difficult to look at him. 'I didn't realise.'

'I didn't mean you to. You do remind me of Helen in a lot of ways, but I don't really see you as a substitute daughter. If you'd accepted my offer, I might well have finished up asking you to marry me.' His smile came again. 'There's no fool like an old fool!'

'You're not old, and you're far from a fool,' Lisa countered. 'You *should* marry again. Only——'

'Only find someone from my own generation,' he finished for her. 'I may do that.' His voice briskened. 'If this is to be our last meal together, we'll make it a good one.'

Lisa couldn't find it in herself to protest as he called over the wine waiter and ordered a bottle of Krug, although she was aware of speculation in the man's eyes. Brett would hear of this apparent celebration, there was no doubt. The rumours would be flying again.

Richard made no attempt to detain her after they finished the meal. He probably would stay on over Christmas, he said in the lobby, if only because there was nowhere else he particularly fancied going. Returning to Boston for the holiday was obviously not an option even to be considered.

On impulse, Lisa kissed him lightly on the cheek before they parted. 'You're a wonderful man, Richard,' she said with sincerity.

'Take care,' he bade her gruffly.

She stood for a contemplative moment looking after him as he moved away, sensing his loneliness. Money might buy a lot of things but it couldn't buy love, and that was what he was missing.

'Try being too clever and you might finish up with nothing,' came the cynical comment, and she turned to meet Gary Conway's regard. He had left the restaurant some time ago; Lisa wondered if he had lingered with purpose.

'I'm not sure what that's supposed to mean,' she said.

'You'll work it out.' He eyed her consideringly. 'How did you manage it?'

Lisa kept her tone even. 'Manage what exactly?'

'Getting Brett to change his mind about having Hanson stay on. And don't try telling me it was nothing to do with you.'

'All right,' she said, 'I won't. If you're so interested, why not ask Brett himself? I'm sure he'd be more than happy to fill you in.'

'It won't last,' Gary returned emphatically. 'You might think you've got him hooked, but you've as much chance of landing him as I have of becoming President!'

Lisa bore down hard on the instinctive retort, settling for flippancy instead. 'Stranger things have happened. Have a nice day, Gary.'

He was right, though, she reflected wryly, going on her way. It would last only as long as Brett wanted it to. The big question was, would she be able to face life here at the Royale when it was over between them?

Busy though she was, the days went by on leaden wings. Felicity came in on Tuesday afternoon, but there was no further approach from Andrea.

The doubts still existed, Lisa was bound to admit, try as she might to dismiss them. The woman had been so utterly sure of herself. Looking back, Brett had shown remarkably little concern over the matter, whereas he should surely have been incensed.

Whatever the truth of it, there was no way of finding out for certain. If she wanted Brett, even on a temporary basis, then she had to disregard the misgivings. And she did want him. More than ever. She could hardly wait to see him again.

His phone call on Wednesday evening gave her a much needed boost. The call would have come through the switchboard, but the possibility of eavesdroppers either hadn't occurred to him or made no impression.

'I've missed you,' he said softly. 'How about you?'

'It's been . . . peaceful,' Lisa answered, and heard his laugh.

'I'll look forward to disrupting it, then. Don't make any plans.'

'You'll be staying over?'

'You bet. It's snowing a blizzard here. I prefer to celebrate in the sun.' He paused. 'Will this be your first Christmas away from home?'

'Yes,' she acknowledged.

'Then we'll have to make up for it.'

Just being with him would make up for it, she yearned to say, but bit it back. At all costs she must keep her cool—give him no cause to believe her any deeper involved than he was himself.

'I can't wait,' she returned lightly.

The pause was lengthier this time, as if he was waiting for her to say something else. 'Me neither,' he responded at length. 'Till Friday, then.'

He had sounded almost disappointed, Lisa thought, replacing the receiver. No doubt other women he knew were adept at verbal flirtation. Perhaps she should start practising herself.

Common sense pointed out the unlikelihood of her developing any skill. Banter of that kind had to be spontaneous. She just wasn't the flirting type.

It rained all Friday morning. It was unusual for it to go on for so long, everyone said, but welcome enough when it came to topping up the holding tanks. Lisa didn't much care what the weather was doing. Tonight she would be seeing Brett again. That was all she could think about.

By seven o'clock, with no word from him as yet, she was beginning to consider the possibility that he had changed his mind about spending Christmas down here. When the call finally came around eight, she was too relieved to dissemble.

'I thought you weren't coming!' she exclaimed.

'Not a chance,' he said, and then on a lightly teasing note, 'Do I take it you'd have been upset if I hadn't?'

Lisa took a hold on her emotions. 'Devastated,' she returned, employing the same tone.

He laughed. 'Have you eaten yet?'

'No.' She added quickly, 'I'm not very hungry.'

'Oddly enough, neither am I.' The pause was timed. 'So?'

To hell with pretence, she thought recklessly. 'I'll be there in five minutes,' she said.

Brett met her on the patio. He was still wearing the suit he had obviously travelled in, Lisa noted fleetingly as he swung her up in his arms. His kiss brought every part of her to tumultuous life, racing the blood through her veins to hammer like crazy in her ears. She clung to him, kissing him back feverishly, wantonly, too overwhelmed to care what she might be giving away...

Some immeasurable time later, Brett put gentle lips to her temple where the hair clung damply.

'I've thought about little else all week but holding you like this—feeling you under me again. Do you have any idea what you do to me, Lisa?'

Her own voice came low and unsteady. 'About the same as you do to me.'

'Tell me what I do to you,' he said softly. 'Tell me what you feel.'

Her heart jerked painfully. He meant in the physical sense, of course.

'Replete,' she got out.

His lips had travelled down her cheek to reach the corner of her mouth, lingering there. 'Just that?'

Lisa struggled to maintain control of her emotions. 'Isn't it enough?'

'I guess it will have to be,' he said after a moment. He kissed her briefly and unsatisfyingly, then lifted

himself away from her, his expression unrevealing.
'Don't go away.'

Lisa came slowly upright as he moved towards the
bathroom. Their clothing lay scattered where it had
landed in those abandoned moments when desire had
overcome finesse for them both. What had he expected
her to say? she wondered. Surely not what she had
wanted so badly to say? The mere mention of love would
change everything. She wasn't prepared to take any risks.

The restraints imposed by the limitations of their relationship put any idea of joining him under the shower
she could now hear running out of the question. She
would need total assurance to indulge in that particular
kind of intimacy, she conceded wryly. 'Don't go away',
he had said, and she wouldn't, but neither was she going
to lie here waiting for him to emerge.

The dark blue dress was badly creased, she saw when
she picked it up from the floor, with the long back zip
come away from the material at the neckline, where Brett
had yanked so urgently at it. Lisa felt warmth run
through her at the memory of her own urgency. Divesting
a man of his clothing was new to her, but she had known
no inhibition. They had been two people possessed by
a common need.

There would be a freshly laundered robe in the guest
bathroom, of course. There always was. Despite her
creeping back to her room in the dawn light the other
morning, the woman who cleaned the house would have
known that Brett hadn't slept alone. Lisa doubted very
much if she would be the first lady friend he had
entertained overnight, but perhaps she was the first employee. That fact alone would account for the degree of
interest engendered among the staff.

Showered, and wearing the towelling robe, she went tentatively back to the bedroom, but Brett wasn't there. She found him seated in the lounge, with coffee ready on a tray. He was wearing a robe too, along with the light leather slippers. Lisa curled her own bare feet under her on the sofa when she took a seat at his side.

'You make wonderful coffee!' she said, tasting the cup he handed her. 'Do you fend for yourself back home in Boston?'

'Apart from coffee and the odd snack, no,' he acknowledged. 'I either eat out or use the hotel restaurant, as I do here.'

'You live in a hotel?'

'I maintain permanent suites in several around the country. That way I can move from place to place with the minimum of palaver.'

'You've never wanted a proper home of your own?' Lisa ventured.

Broad shoulders lifted. 'This place is the nearest I've come to it, I suppose. Not that I normally spend as much time here as I have done these past few weeks.'

Lisa kept her eyes on the cup in her hand. 'So I gathered.'

The pause stretched between them. Brett broke the silence with an exasperated sigh. 'You're doing the chameleon act again!'

'No, I'm not.' She still couldn't look at him directly. 'I'm not sure what you want me to say.'

He took the cup from her and replaced it in its saucer, turning back again to take her by the shoulders and bring her round to face him. The grey eyes had glittering green specks in them. 'I want you to tell me what I really am to you!'

She gazed back at him in confusion, unprepared for the sudden switch in attitude.

'I don't see you as a meal ticket, if that's what you're getting at,' she said. 'I'm not interested in your money, Brett.'

The hands on her shoulders tautened as if they were about to shake her. 'I'm talking about how you feel, for God's sake!'

She swallowed thickly. 'I told you that earlier.'

'You told me nothing apart from what I already knew. Sure I can satisfy you physically! I'd take an early retirement if I failed in that department.' He paused, eyes searching hers with an intensity that started a cautious glow deep inside her. 'You know damn well what I'm asking!'

'It cuts both ways,' she said on a husky note. 'How do *you* feel?'

'Like hell,' he growled. 'The way I've felt all week. No woman ever intruded on my working hours the way you've done.'

The glow had increased; Lisa damped it down with an effort, still not sure where all this was heading. The word had to come from him, if it came from anyone, but she would go partway.

'No man ever intruded on mine before either,' she admitted. 'I never wanted any other man this way.'

'Only want?' His voice had softened along with his hands, the latter moving inwards and upwards to cup her face. 'I need more than that from you.'

Lisa quivered as his lips touched hers. The tenderness in that kiss was her undoing. She gave her emotions free rein, clinging to him, whispering the words against his mouth. The relief in letting go at last was cathartic.

'*That's* what I wanted to hear,' he said roughly. He looked deep into her eyes, his expression serious. 'You'd better mean it.'

She returned his regard unflinchingly. 'I never meant anything more.'

Something in him seemed to relax. He kissed her again, held her close. 'I'd given up hope of ever feeling this way about any woman.'

'Which way?' she asked, and he gave a low laugh.

'Like life isn't worth living when you're not around to share it with. How do you feel about marrying me?' He held her away from him when she failed to reply, lips twisting as he registered her expression. 'Is it such a bad idea?'

'No.' Her voice was uneven. 'Just unexpected. It's barely a month since we met.'

'So what? The important thing is how we feel now, not how long it took to get there.'

'You said compatibility was more important than love,' Lisa murmured.

'I always thought so. I still consider it pretty vital, but we've no problems on that score.'

'Are we compatible?' she asked doubtfully.

'In every sense, I'd say.'

'There's more to marriage than bed.'

'I'm sure.' The smile was in his eyes too. 'A whole lot more. I'm not saying there won't be disagreements. Life would be very dull if we shared every opinion. And, having waited this long, I'm not prepared to wait too much longer either,' he added firmly. 'We can bring your whole family out, and be married right here.'

Lisa was too dazed still to think straight. 'You mean at the Royale?'

'We've held weddings before. Naturally, we wouldn't be spending the honeymoon here.'

'We've already had the honeymoon,' she murmured.

He shook his head. 'No, we haven't. Lovemaking is only a part of it. I want to spend premium time with you, Lisa. Somewhere we can't be reached.'

Eyes luminous, she said softly, 'You'd ignore your business commitments?'

'I'd delegate.'

He searched her face, then drew her to him again, running his hands possessively through her hair as he kissed her long and deep. Lisa responded with heart and soul, overwhelmed. It was happening the way she had dreamed about, the way she had yearned for. There would never, she thought, be another moment to match this.

They made love again, right there on the sofa, proving her wrong because each and every moment was more consummate than the last. It was only afterwards, when she lay holding the proud dark head on her breast, that other matters began to impinge on her consciousness.

'What about *my* work?' she asked softly. 'Would you expect me to give it up?'

Brett didn't lift his head. 'Not unless you wanted to. You can open your own salon. You'd find a ready market for your talents in Boston.' He paused, breath warm against her skin. 'Providing it didn't take over your life.'

'I can't let you finance a salon for me,' she protested.

'Why on earth not? Do you think I'd let my wife work for a salary?' He shifted position to look up at her, his expression amused. 'I can afford it.'

'I know.' She made a helpless little gesture. 'It's going to take some getting used to.'

'You'll cope.' He said it with conviction. 'We'll still be coming down here on occasion, of course, but there are other places I want to take you. We'll both have to learn to delegate from time to time.'

'If you can, I can.' Lisa gave a sigh of pure happiness. 'I still keep thinking I'm going to wake up and find this is all a dream!'

'It's real enough,' he assured her. A wicked glint sprang in his eyes. 'So am I.'

Her responses as his lips discovered a whole new erogenous zone were real enough too. She could never have too much of this, she thought ecstatically. Life had never been as good.

They spent the night together, of course. Only this time Brett refused to let her leave first thing.

'Nothing we do is anyone else's business unless it affects them directly,' he stated at breakfast. 'In fact, why not move up here wholesale?'

The idea was tempting, Lisa was bound to admit. Yet there was still a barrier.

'When do you plan on announcing things?' she asked diffidently, and saw his expression undergo a subtle change.

'Is there any hurry?'

'Well, no, of course not.' She hesitated before continuing, 'I'd just feel more comfortable, I suppose.'

'On the premise that sharing a bed with a fiancé is less of a talking point?'

The sardonic note stirred a sudden resentment. 'As a matter of fact, yes,' she returned shortly. 'It may be a silly attitude in your eyes, but I can't help that. Why keep it a secret anyway?'

There was a lengthy pause as Brett studied her reflectively, then he shrugged. 'No particular reason. I'll put the word out right away.'

Lisa bit her lip, already regretting the acrimony. 'I wasn't trying to put pressure on you,' she said. 'I know that's what it must have sounded like, but I really didn't mean it that way.'

He smiled briefly. 'However you meant it, it's a valid point. Why keep quiet about it?'

On impulse, Lisa got up from her seat and went round the table to slide her arms over his shoulders from the rear and press her cheek to his. 'I'm sorry,' she murmured ruefully. 'I was just being stupid.'

Brett reached up an arm and drew her round and down across his lap. His smile lacked its former restraint, warming his eyes again. 'No, you weren't. I was the one at fault.'

She widened her eyes at him in mock-astonishment. 'Brett Sanderson at fault? Never!'

'Carry on that way and you'll find yourself up-ended,' he threatened.

Laughing, Lisa kissed him, thrilling as always to the feel of his lips against hers. Love was so wonderful when it was returned. She felt as if she owned the whole world!

It was gone eleven before she went down to start packing her things. Running into Gary was sheer fate, she supposed. That he had a very good idea where she was coming from was obvious.

'Sleep well?' he asked sarcastically.

Lisa kept her expression strictly neutral. 'Very, thanks. Did you?'

'I didn't have anything to keep me awake,' he said. 'Don't forget to hang up your stocking tonight.'

'I'd hardly forget Christmas, even if it is eighty degrees,' she returned mildly. She added on impulse, 'Seeing it is Christmas, can't we bury the hatchet and be friends again, Gary? I'm eternally in your debt for having given me this opportunity in the first place. If it weren't for you, I'd——'

'If it weren't for me, you'd still be looking for some other sucker,' he came back harshly. 'Don't try making out that my opinion matters to you.'

'I never took you for a sucker,' Lisa protested. 'Whatever you might have imagined, I gave you no cause to think I might be interested in anything more than the job.'

There was no softening of his expression. 'Sure you didn't. Butter wouldn't melt in your mouth!' He made an impatient gesture as she started to speak. 'Don't waste your breath. Your time will come. Maybe sooner than you think.'

The news was going to shock him to the core, thought Lisa wryly as he turned away. She would gain no pleasure from it either.

Brett had suggested she pack her things and leave her suitcases to be taken up to the house while they were out to lunch. He hadn't said where they would be going, although she had gathered that they wouldn't be eating here. It would be as well, she thought, if she told him about seeing Richard on Sunday, before he heard it from anyone else, although now they had everything straight between them it hardly mattered any more.

The arrangement had been that Brett would pick her up out front in the car at twelve-thirty. Wearing a peach linen trouser suit, she was applying lipstick when the door opened without warning. Brett looked across at her with a stony expression.

'Just how much is your word worth?' he asked harshly.

Lisa put down the lipstick, trying to keep a cool head. Gary obviously hadn't wasted any time. 'If we're talking about my seeing Richard on Sunday, I was going to tell you myself.'

'You've had plenty of opportunity.'

'Not really.' She attempted to lighten the moment with a smile. 'I had other things to think about.'

The curl of his upper lip sent her heart plummeting. She tried again, her voice appealing for reason. 'I only saw him that once to tell him to his face why I couldn't see him again.'

'You were drinking champagne,' he said. 'That doesn't sound much like a farewell party.'

'That's exactly *what* it was.'

'Like hell! I should have had more sense than to ever take in that "just good friends" story you gave me. He's had you too, hasn't he?'

'That's not true!' She was desperate to convince him. 'Richard was never more than a friend. He never could have been!'

'So you say. Except that I don't believe a word of it.' His tone was all the more lacerating for its very control. 'He's welcome to you. I'm opting out.'

Lisa stood there frozen as the door closed. If last night had been a dream, this was a nightmare! What price his professed love if he thought her capable of such behaviour? she thought numbly. She had accepted his word over Andrea.

It was some time before she could gain enough control of her emotions to consider where she went from here. Staying on after this was out of the question; she doubted anyway if Brett would allow her to keep her job. Her bags were packed, and she still had her return ticket.

Providing she could get on a flight, she could be home by this time tomorrow. Running away, perhaps, but what alternative did she have?

Action was an anodyne of sorts. A phone call to one of the downtown agencies secured her a seat on the three o'clock shuttle to San Juan, and another on a flight leaving for New York at six-thirty. She was going to be stuck there until nine o'clock Christmas morning, and wouldn't be landing in England until early evening, but it was the best they could do for her.

It was still only one o'clock now, she realised, glancing at her watch as she replaced the receiver. That gave her ample time to reach the airport, even allowing for the holiday festivities already hotting up in the town. She had no intention of leaving any message for Brett. Let him draw his own conclusions.

So far she was managing to keep her emotions at bay, though the pain would win through eventually, Lisa knew. She changed out of the peach trouser suit into a more practical dark blue one, then rang to order a taxi, dismayed to be told it would be half an hour at least before one was available. Making the usual allowances for Caribbean time, she was probably going to be cutting it fine after all, she acknowledged hollowly, but there was nothing she could do about it. She would just have to sit and wait.

Some forty minutes only had gone by when the phone rang. Surprised, but relieved too, Lisa picked it up to say, 'I'll be right out.'

'It's Richard,' came the reply. 'I couldn't leave without at least wishing you a happy Christmas, Lisa.'

'You're leaving today?' she said blankly.

'That's right. I decided last night. I'm going to spend Christmas in Boston with my son and his family.'

'That's good.' She tried to infuse some genuine feeling into her voice. 'It's the best place to be.'

'There's something wrong, isn't there?' he said. 'Brett still playing you around?'

Her laugh was brittle. 'Not for much longer. I'm leaving too. I'm on the three o'clock shuttle to San Juan.'

'Has he told you to go?'

'I'm saving him the trouble.'

'I see.' Richard's tone altered. 'Is this anything to do with me?'

'Nothing your fault.' Lisa already regretted having said as much as she had. 'Forget it, Richard. It isn't important. Have a wonderful Christmas, and take care of yourself.'

She hung up before he could say anything else. There was nothing else *to* say. All she wanted now was to be home again. One place she wouldn't be looking for a job in the new year was the salon she had left so blithely a month ago. A new start was what she needed.

It was two o'clock before a taxi became available. Even then, she was sharing it with a group going down to the town. The sun beat down out of a clear blue sky, highlighting the familiar, achingly beautiful panorama. She was going to miss all this, Lisa was bound to admit. Who wouldn't? If only things could have been different.

The town was thronged, traffic moving at a snail's pace. A steel band was playing on the waterfront, with limbo dancers and fire-eaters entertaining the crowds. Despite the heat, the Christmas spirit abounded. Tonight would be one great party.

They made the airport with only twenty minutes to spare, the flight itself bare seconds before it was due to take off. Sinking into her seat, Lisa closed her eyes and kept them closed, unwilling to take a last look at the island. That phase of her life was over.

She sat around for over an hour at San Juan waiting for the New York flight check-in desk to open so that she could get rid of her luggage. With that done, she still had two hours to get through. There was a cafeteria on the main concourse. Not in the least bit hungry, but recognising the need for sustenance of some kind, she settled for coffee and a doughnut, and sat listlessly in the window watching the comings and goings.

The cafeteria was busy, all seats occupied. A young couple with a child in a carry-cot shared her table for a while. They wished her a merry Christmas on leaving. Lisa summoned a smile and an equable reply, then turned her face back to the window, not bothering to look round again when someone else slid into the vacated seat next to her.

'I was beginning to think you'd already left,' said Brett levelly.

Lisa's head came round as if pulled on a string, eyes dark as she surveyed the firm features of the man she loved. Her heart felt as if it might break out through her ribcage any moment.

'What are you doing here?' she asked huskily.

'I've come to fetch you back,' he said. 'And to apologise for going off the top the way I did.' His lips twisted. 'I wasn't thinking straight at the time.'

'And you are now?'

'With some help from Hanson.'

Her breath caught. 'You've spoken to Richard?'

'He did most of the speaking.' Brett glanced at the man seated opposite, who was listening with interest to the conversation, and added decisively, 'Let's get out of here.'

Lisa allowed herself to be drawn from her seat, moving like an automaton in their progress to the door. She could hardly believe this was actually happening. In another moment she would waken up on the plane and realise it was just another dream.

Only there was nothing dream-like about the warmth and firmness of the hand under her elbow. Brett threaded his way purposefully through the milling throng to seek out a quiet corner out of sight and sound of the general mêlée and take her in his arms, kissing her with a passion and thoroughness that obliterated every remaining doubt from her mind.

'I love you,' he said roughly, holding her close. 'I love you, I want you and I need you, Lisa!'

'But do you trust me?' she whispered shakily. 'Do you really believe I never made love with Richard?'

'Yes. I was blind with jealousy when Gary told me about seeing the two of you together last Sunday so soon after I left. I wanted to hurt you the way I was hurting.' His lips were at her temple, his hands strong at her back. 'I'd cooled down by the time Hanson dropped in on me. Enough to realise what a fool I'd been. As he said, I've known too many of Andrea Gordon's ilk.'

Lisa looked up into the grey eyes, telling herself that trust should be mutual but still unable to put the other woman aside that easily. 'About Andrea——'

'I told you the truth,' he said. 'There was never any question of marriage between us.'

'But you have been ... lovers?'

Brett returned her regard levelly. 'I can't pretend to have been a monk. All I can tell you is there's been nothing between us since you came on the scene. Nor, if it comes to that, has there been anyone else.'

She relaxed with a sigh. 'I'm glad. I hate to think of you making love to another woman.'

'There won't be any others. Not when I have you to come home to.' His tone roughened again. 'We're going to have a long-term marriage, with trust on both sides. The kind of marriage our children can feel secure in too.'

Commitment was the word, thought Lisa mistily as he drew her to him again. Not just this Christmas, but all those to come.

10th anniversary

Temptation is Ten!

Join the festivities as Mills & Boon celebrates Temptation's tenth anniversary in February 1995.

There's a whole host of in-book competitions and special offers with some great prizes to be won—watch this space for more details!

In March, we have a sizzling new mini-series Lost Loves about love lost...love found. And, of course, the Temptation range continues to offer you fun, sensual exciting stories all year round.

After ten tempting years, nobody can resist

Temptation 10th anniversary

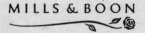

Next Month's Romances

Each month you can choose from a wide variety of romance with Mills & Boon. Below are the new titles to look out for next month, why not ask either Mills & Boon Reader Service or your Newsagent to reserve you a copy of the titles you want to buy – just tick the titles you would like and either post to Reader Service or take it to any Newsagent and ask them to order your books.

Please save me the following titles: Please tick

Title	Author	✓
BURNING WITH PASSION	*Emma Darcy*	
THE WRONG KIND OF WIFE	*Roberta Leigh*	
RAW SILK	*Anne Mather*	
ONE NIGHT OF LOVE	*Sally Wentworth*	
THUNDER ON THE REEF	*Sara Craven*	
INVITATION TO LOVE	*Leigh Michaels*	
VENGEFUL BRIDE	*Rosalie Ash*	
DARK OASIS	*Helen Brooks*	
YESTERDAY'S HUSBAND	*Angela Devine*	
TAINTED LOVE	*Alison Fraser*	
NO PLACE FOR LOVE	*Susanne McCarthy*	
THAT DEVIL LOVE	*Lee Wilkinson*	
SHINING THROUGH	*Barbara McMahon*	
MANDATE FOR MARRIAGE	*Catherine O'Connor*	
DESERT MAGIC	*Mons Daveson*	
DANGEROUS FLIRTATION	*Liz Fielding*	

If you would like to order these books in addition to your regular subscription from Mills & Boon Reader Service please send £1.90 per title to: Mills & Boon Reader Service, Freepost, P.O. Box 236, Croydon, Surrey, CR9 9EL, quote your Subscriber No:................................... (if applicable) and complete the name and address details below. Alternatively, these books are available from many local Newsagents including W H Smith, J Menzies, Martins and other paperback stockists from 10 February 1995.

Name:..

Address:..

...............................Post Code:........................

To Retailer: If you would like to stock M&B books please contact your regular book/magazine wholesaler for details.

You may be mailed with offers from other reputable companies as a result of this application. If you would rather not take advantage of these opportunities please tick box. ☐